BUILT TO LAST
A LIFETIME

A NOVEL OF OLD KENTUCKY

BOOK THREE
TRAVELERS ON THE TRAIL

BOOK FOUR
THE RIVER RUNS WIDE

ELIZABETH DURBIN
AND
ERNEST MATUSCHKA

Elizabeth Durbin

BUILT TO LAST A LIFETIME
VOLUME TWO

© Copyright 2005
Elizabeth Durbin, Ernest Matuschka through
the writing partnership of Durmat Associates
ISBN #0-911041-36-2

Published for Durmat Associates by
OPA Publishing
Box 12354
Chandler, AZ 85248-0023

opa

TABLE OF CONTENTS - BOOK THREE
TRAVELERS ON THE TRAIL

TABLE OF CONTENTS - BOOK FOUR
THE RIVER RUNS WIDE

INTRODUCTION

To the Reader:

This is a novel of old Kentucky, set in the late 1700s or early 1800s, at about the same time that Daniel Boone was making his reputation. It was a time when people from the eastern states could move into the Kentucky territory and stake a claim on land, provided that they built a shelter, cleared some land, and raised a crop. This is a historical novel, which means that the history and setting are accurate but the people are fictional. The dialect used in this book reflects the language style that was spoken by the early settler in Kentucky. It should be noted that while there is adventure in this book, there is a minimum of descriptive violence and an absence of sexual content. It is written for young people in middle-school or for high school students who may enjoy a book of high interest and lower vocabulary levels.

CHAPTER ONE

READY TO SETTLE

"Luke," said Adam Blake, "I've been all over this Kentucky County, from the mountains to the big river west, and I haven't seen any place that I like better than right around here. When you have time, I'd appreciate your helping me mark off a place to settle before all the good places are gone." The two frontiersmen were sitting in front of a blazing fire at Luke's cabin.

Luke nodded. "I would be most happy to help you get started, Adam. I believe there's a parcel of land about five miles from here that is worth a look."

Mouthwatering odors rose from the big, black Dutch oven hanging over the flames in the fireplace. The pungent fragrances rose through the sturdy chimney that Luke had built when he first moved his family to the wilderness. Their first cabin had been burned down when Indians raided the homestead and captured his daughter Sarah. She had survived her capture by the Indians, and on this day she had prepared the stew that bubbled in the pot. Sarah was wise in the use of herbs and edible roots. As a result, Luke, Nathan and Lucas were better fed than most settlers. Sarah had learned many useful things from the Indian women she lived and worked with during the months she had been a captive.

Nathan, her brother, had also been captured and, like Sarah, had spent much time learning hunting and fishing skills from the Indians. It was he who had speared the small game that was to be their dinner. Shot and powder were scarce on the frontier. Nathan's skill with snares, slings and traps that he made himself were helpful in keeping the family in fresh meat.

Sarah, Nathan and Luke, their father, were the only members of the family still alive. Gone—victims of the savage Indian attack—were Gramma, the mother of Luke's deceased wife Lizabeth, and two infant siblings, a boy and a girl whom the Indians thought too young to be brought back to their camp as slaves.

Life was difficult in the wilderness. Not only were the Indians still a danger, but also only the very strong were able to withstand the illnesses, weather and hardships with which they had to contend. The dwindling family had acquired a new member when Lucas joined them two springs before. He was an orphaned boy whose parents had been killed in an Indian raid, leaving him captive at a very young age. It was believed that after Lucas' parents were killed he had been taken by the Indians and raised for about six years as one of their own. Since he had spent so much of his life among the savages, Lucas believed himself to be an Indian in spite of his blue eyes and blond hair.

It was only after many captives were recovered from the tribe that Lucas' real identity became known. It was found that he was a child who had been searched for by his remaining family, well-to-do Easterners who had almost given him up for dead.

His snobbish uncle, Henry Peabody, accompanied by his half-brother, Adam Blake, had come to investigate the appearance of a boy believed to be that child, but Mr. Peabody ultimately rejected the notion that Lucas was his nephew. Consequently, Lucas was welcomed into the current family, and happily so.

As Adam had explained to Lucas, Lucas' father and Henry Peabody were brothers. Therefore, Adam was also a half brother to Lucas's father, since they both shared the same mother.

All of this was very confusing to young Lucas, who had accepted Luke as his father and Nathan and Sarah as his true brother and sister.

After Henry Peabody rejected Lucas as his nephew, Claiming, erroneously, that Luke was attempting to defraud him in an attempt to get money, Peabody returned to Boston. However, Adam was so entranced with this beautiful country that he decided to stay on, and he also decided that he wanted to settle near Luke. Adam had no desire to return to Boston, nor did Lucas. Adam preferred the wild beauty and challenge of the frontier. Now he was ready to lay claim to the land and establish a home.

Delia, a younger sister to Adam, had remained in Boston while her brother and her older half-brother journeyed to the Kentucky frontier. She patiently waited, hoping that when Adam had completed his wanderings he would be ready to settle down in their familiar New England environment. When she received word that he had found a beautiful place in Kentucky that suited him, she almost immediately changed her plan and began preparing to join him. Delia, too, had the pioneer spirit and found herself longing to know more about the west. After all, she thought, she was less enthusiastic about leaving calling cards and drinking tea with genteel ladies whose only concerns were with fashions and gossip than she was about learning new things and going to new places.

After the meal was finished, Luke said, "Tomorrow, Nathan and I plan to hunt in the general direction of the land you are interested in. It's only a few miles from us here, so we'll be close neighbors."

"I appreciate that, Luke. We can all look at the land, and you can advise me as to the boundaries.

"We both know the land and there are some parcels that lay right good."

Nathan added, "Adam, it is a beautiful parcel of land."

Luke continued, "We can start in the morning. I ain't heard of troubles with the Indians since we raided their village and got our captives back, but still I don't want to leave Sarah alone. Lucas, will you stay with Sarah?"

Lucas, who wanted to go but wouldn't disappoint Luke, responded, "Yes, Pa, I will."

"Sarah is more valuable to the Indians now that she is almost grown," Luke said.

"That sounds like a good plan to me," Adam responded. "We can see the land and I can help pack the meat back."

After Sarah had finished cleaning up after supper, she sat down next to Adam who was carving an axe handle out of wood. She said. "Adam, tell me about Delia."

Adam grinned with pride. "Oh, Sarah, you will love Delia! She has the true pioneer's spirit. She is adventuresome and well suited to live in the wilderness. Neither of us matched well with Henry's Boston."

"I mean, what does she look like?"

"Well, I think she is pretty. She is maybe an inch or so taller than you. She is a bit heavier because she is a grown woman. She's twenty years old. She has long, light brown hair and brown eyes. Her eyes are a window to her feelings. Most of the time she has soft brown eyes filled with love. But when she is angry she . . . I mean, her eyes flash with fire, maybe even lightning!"

"But she *is* educated, Adam. Do you think an educated woman will want to be in the wilderness?"

"Yes, Delia was a very good student. She had high marks in school in Boston. She also went to college for, I think, two years. She wanted to be a teacher. As to how happy she'll be out here . . . well, that's anybody's guess."

"I'll do my part to make her happy. I do want to have another woman to talk to."

Sarah blushed at the reference of herself as a woman.

"I know you will, Sarah, and I know that you and Delia will become close friends."

Not too far away sat Lucas, listening intently and absorbing everything.

CHAPTER TWO

A HOME FOR ADAM

They broke through a grove of trees onto a bluff of sandstone that overlooked a broad panorama of overwhelming beauty. Adam gasped, "Luke, look! The trees cover miles and miles, as far as I can see!"

It was a gorgeous sight. Streams wandered through the bottomland, giving promise of plenty of water for the animals that would use them.

"This is unusual, Adam. Most stone hereabouts is limestone. Some folks call this place the Devil's Side Saddle. Look how the rocks crop out on three sides, sort of like a seat."

"I never saw such moss as this growing on the rocks, Luke. Looks almost like the coral the sea captains in Boston bring back from the South Seas. It is interesting stuff. I'm wondering if Sarah could find a use for it. That girl could find a use for the squeal from a pig if she had a pig around," observed Adam.

"I don't rightly know how Sarah could use the moss. But I know that if she wanted a pig, Sam'l would probably find a way to get her one. He spoils that girl somethin' awful," said Luke.

"Once he said that Sarah reminded him of Becka, a girl that he was engaged to. Then he clammed up and wouldn't say any more. He just got a sort of lonely, faraway look in his eyes," Nathan added.

"Sometimes I worry about Sam'l. He is such a loner. He hunts, traps and fishes and can turn his hand to anything you need. I've known him ever since we were settled, but I can't say I know any more about his past today than I did the day I met him. He keeps everything to himself." Luke shook his head.

"Well, Pa, he sure has helped us. He seems to sense what we need and just show up with it. I guess we don't need to know about his past if he don't want to talk about it. He is a good friend. That's all that matters."

"You're partly right, Nathan. I still see a lonely man, but I shouldn't have to have a lesson in trust where Sam'l is concerned. I don't know what we'd have done if he wasn't there to help us," Luke admitted. "Let's go back over that knoll. Seems like there's a good place to put up a cabin. If I remember right, there's a stream that runs through the bottom over there. Maybe we'll see signs of deer, too."

The three of them walked through the woods, leaving hardly any signs that they'd been there. The young lime-green leaves on the trees scarcely stirred as they passed, and without thinking about it, each of them carefully placed his feet so as not to leave a trail. They were accustomed to a caution that had become second nature to them. They communicated with signs rather than words, and, because of the buckskins they wore, they seemed to fade into the brush.

Soon they reached the stream. In silent agreement, they scouted both sides of it for danger. Reassured, they met at a flat rock to decide where to build a cabin.

"This is an ideal spot, Luke."

"It looks real good to me, too, Adam."

As Adam and Luke talked about the land and how it was situated, Nathan took a line and hook from his pouch. He turned over several rocks at the edge of the stream and picked up the crawfish he unearthed. After threading one on his hook, he tossed it into the water and waited for a fish to be tempted. A fish wrapped in leaves and steamed to tender doneness appealed to his always-present hunger. Sarah had said that she spent half her time cooking enough to feed him and the other half getting enough food to cook for him.

He knew that Sarah was anxious for Pa to get a deer today. Nathan had outgrown his clothes. To make him new ones, she needed more skins to replace those she had already used. He was about to split out of the buckskins he wore. She could save the outgrown garments for Lucas. He, too, was growing and would fit into Nathan's clothing in a few years. They could afford to waste nothing.

"This looks like a likely place for a homestead, Luke. The deer sign is plentiful, and we have seen many small critters. I'm grateful to you for finding this spot for me."

"I'm happy to do it for you, Adam. It's mighty lonely out here in the wilderness without neighbors close by."

"Let's begin marking the boundaries before dark. I'm anxious to get started and to lay claim to this land."

"If we get a deer first thing in the morning, we can cut some poles and put up a shelter while it's bleedin' out," Luke said as he stood up and made a small pile of rocks as the first marker on Adam's claim. "I wonder if Nathan caught any fish for supper."

As Adam crested the first hill beyond the stream, Nathan held up two nice sized fish. He said, "Now don't go catching all of them. Save some for my sister when she gets here." Adam laughed and set up a second pile of stones for the boundary.

CHAPTER THREE

THE GIFT BEARER

"Here comes Sam'l. Wonder what he's bringing this trip," called Lucas as he looked up from the row of corn he was planting.

Sarah was sweeping the floor with sand brought up from the creek bottom. It made the floor white and smooth. It was her pride and joy. Not many cabins had floors of wood. When Pa and Nathan had rebuilt the cabin after the raid, they had replaced everything just as it had been when Ma and Gramma were alive. Sarah vowed to keep it as clean as they had. It was hard to do with Nathan and Lucas tracking in and out all of the time. Pa was almost as bad as they were.

She straightened up and saw Sam'l talking to Pa. She sighed. Sam'l was worse than her three put together, she mused. He lived alone in a cabin that was in not much better shape than a lean-to. It never occurred to him to scrape his feet before he came inside. He'd sit by the fire and whittle at some tool handle or stirring stick, letting the wood chips fall anywhere. Often, when he'd finished eating, he would toss a bone across the room to Digger. He'd laugh when the dog missed catching it. Of course, he always left plenty of meat on it for the dog to enjoy. Sarah would have the job of getting the grease stains off the sand-whitened boards.

She shook herself and muttered; "Sarah, you sound ungrateful. Sam'l was always thinking of you and bringing you something nice." She knew she should be grateful for his friendship. She just wished he were a little neater.

She stood and straightened her drab but clean dress. Her blond hair was neatly drawn back from her face into a single, thick braid fastened with a leather throng. On her feet were moccasins, made from the skins of deer, which she had scraped and tanned. Her hands, clean and well-formed but callused from the harsh work, were rarely still. Even when she finished her daily chores, she kept busy with the endless mending and knitting that was necessary to keep clothed and warm. Everything they used or wore had to be made from whatever was available from the land on which they lived.

Sarah went to the fireplace and stirred the simmering stew. There was always plenty for them to eat. She had known hunger, and she was pleased to know that she now had food enough prepared for an unexpected guest. She decided to make corn cakes because Sam'l liked them so much. He rarely bothered to cook anything except what he could roast over an open fire, and then just enough to nourish his body.

She could see that he had put his pack aside and was helping with the planting. With his help, they would finish much sooner than they had expected.

Sam'l came to visit often and was always willing to lend a helping hand at whatever task was in progress. His strength was welcome, and he was skilled in the needs of the frontier. As a woodsman, there was no one more able than Sam'l at stalking and providing game. He never came empty handed. Although he was a large man, he could move through the woods without making a sound. His buckskins made him appear to melt into the woods, and his skin and hair blended so well with the brown of the skins he wore they could barely be seen.

✄

"Sarah, I do believe that you are the best cook in the world." Sam'l pushed his stool back from the table. "If I ate your cookin' every day, I'd be so fat someone would shoot me for a grizzly bear just wakin' up from his winter's sleep."

Sarah blushed at Sam'l's compliment.

"Have you seen any bear signs around, Sam'l?" Luke asked. "I'd like to find one. The skin sure would be good to have in the winter, and Sarah could use the fat for her soap makin'."

"Not around here I haven't seen many. But I know a place towards the mountains in the east where there's plenty of bear. Maybe Adam will want to go with me and get a skin or two for his sister," Sam'l replied. "We can take the extra meat to the settlement. They can always use it."

"His sister!" Sarah cried. "When did she get here? Where is she? What's she like? How?..."

"Whoa! Sarah. She ain't here yet. She's comin' with the next wagon train of settlers. Feller rode into the settlement the other day and said they was comin' through the pass now that the snow was melted. They should be here in about a month. That's why I came out this way. I've got to warn Adam she's comin'."

"Oh, Pa, can she stay with us? Adam ain't had time to build a proper cabin yet. I ain't talked to a woman since we were at the fort when you brought us back. Please, Pa, please. She can have my bed, I'll sleep on the floor," begged Sarah. "I'd better get started cleaning up this place."

"Now, calm down, daughter. Of course she's welcome here. We'll ask her, but she'll have to decide for herself what she wants to do. As for you givin' up your bed, we'll see. I've been thinkin' on adding a dogtrot and another room to the cabin. We're getting' mighty crowded the way the boys are growin'. If I can talk Sam'l into stayin' over a couple of days, maybe he can help raise the walls and beams for the roof. With four men working on it and you chinkin' the logs, it shouldn't take long. I've been savin' logs and squarin' them off back up in the woods. I wanted to surprise you."

"You sure did! I love you, Pa." Sarah jumped up and hugged Luke.

"I've got a surprise for you, too, but it ain't as good as that," Sam'l added. "Guess I don't get a hug," he teased.

"Sure you do, Sam'l." Sarah ran over to him and hugged him. Sam'l face turned red and he looked embarrassed as he groped in his pack for his gift.

Sarah also blushed, surprised by her own exuberance.

"It ain't much, Sarah. That feller I told you about bringin' news of Adam's sister had it in his pack. He was usin' it for tradin' purposes. I traded him a few things he needed for it. Then I didn't know what to do with it—'til I thought about you." Sam'l was still flustered.

His big hand completely enclosed what was in it. Sarah was alive with curiosity. What could he have for her that he could hide in his hand?

Finally, he placed his gift on the table. It was wrapped in a piece of cloth.

"Here it is, Sarah, but what use you'd have for it I don't know." Sam'l backed away, as though fearful of getting another hug.

Carefully, Sarah unwrapped the cloth. Inside lay a lady's watch attached to a gold bow pin. It had been designed to be worn on a dress. Sarah had never seen anything so beautiful. She looked at Sam'l with eyes shining with tears. Just a few hours ago she had been fussing because he made a mess, now he presented her with this wonderful gift. She didn't know what to say.

Finally, speaking over the lump in her throat, she said, "Oh, Sam'l, this is far too good for me. You should save it for the girl you're going to marry someday. It's so beautiful." Immediately, Sarah realized what she had said and blushed deeply.

Sam'l answered, "That ain't likely to happen. You keep it, Sarah. Maybe some day you'll have a place to wear it. I ain't got no need of a wife." His manner warned her not to ask questions.

Confused, she simply said, "Thank you, Sam'l. I'll treasure this forever."

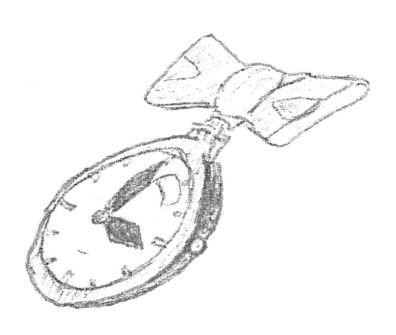

CHAPTER FOUR

GETTING READY
FOR COMPANY

"That's the last of the roof beams. Again, Sam'l, I don't know what we'd do without your help." Luke said as he stepped back to look at the new room and dog trot.

The new addition would almost double the living space of the original cabin and would provide privacy for Sarah, and for Delia when she came.

"I'll get the shingles made, and the boys and I will put them on before Adam's sister gets here. I've got a few already cut, so that will help. If the weather holds good, it won't be a problem getting them on. If it don't, we'll just double up and try not to get in each other's way," Luke said as he walked to the water pail to get a drink from the gourd dipper.

Sarah toiled up the hill from the stream, carrying an oaken bucket of water in each hand. She was getting ready to wash clothes. She pushed her hair back from her face and poured water into the big, black iron kettle that hung over the fire outside the cabin. The clothes she planned to wash needed hot water. For things less soiled, she went to the creek and pounded out the dirt by laying the clothes on a rock and beating the dirt out with a paddle. It was hard work to stay clean. It was even harder work to convince Lucas and Nathan to get clean. It wasn't too bad when the weather was warm and they could swim and wash off the dirt. But when it got cold, they avoided washing themselves as much as possible. The only way she could get them to bathe was by bribing them with food. Either of them would do anything for a sweet treat.

"Seein' Sarah carryin' water reminds me of somethin' I've been meaning to tell you about," Sam'l recalled. "Same feller I got the watch from said something about Martha needin' a rain barrel. We used to have one back east, I remember, to catch the rainwater for washin' and such. The way Sarah keeps drainin' the creek for water to wash everythin', she could use one up here."

"Leave it to you Sam'l, to think of such a handy thing. You sure would make a good husband for some deserving woman," Luke observed.

Sam'l's face shut down. Abruptly, he turned away from Luke and busied himself with sharpening the blade on his axe.

Finally, Sam'l asked, "Do you have some good oak cut and seasonin'? A good way into the woods I saw a tree that would do for the barrel. Oak's best for holdin' water. I'll cut the tree and prop it to season, then when I come back we can cut it into boards and shape them into staves."

"Well, don't tell Sarah. She'll have me stop the plowin' and plantin' to make her a barrel. She won't be patient for the wood to get right," Luke cautioned. "If it has anythin' to do with makin' it easier for her to keep things clean, she won't let up until she gets it."

"She's the cleanest girl I ever saw. Last night, after we ate, when I was makin' a new handle for Lucas's axe, she kept sweepin' up the wood shavin's before they hit the floor," Sam'l chuckled. "Wood shavin's ain't even dirty."

Luke and Sam'l walked to the edge of the clearing. "I wish I could go over and help Adam get the ground cleared for his cabin, but I can't right now," Luke said.

"I was thinkin' of helping him get the ground cleared for a crop. He's got a lean-to. As long as that sister of his can stay here with you for a spell, that's all he needs. But he really should get a crop of corn in so he has some food for the winter.

"I reckon that is much more important for him. He can always build the cabin in his spare time. The lean to is his shelter, but he has to have a crop the first year to file for his claim."

"I hope Delia can put up with the way we live out here" replied Sam'l. "Surely, Adam's told her life out here ain't fancy like she's used to in the city." Sam'l shrugged his shoulders and headed into the trees.

"I just hope she doesn't have any city notions. She won't last long out here if she thinks she'll be waited on," Luke observed. "I don't want her givin' Sarah any fancy ideas, either."

CHAPTER FIVE

PRINCESS

"**P**a! We got the shingles on the new room and the corn planted. Can we go over to help Adam today?" Nathan asked. "I saw him hunting yesterday, and he said that he had a field cleared. If it was dry enough, he wanted to break ground. Since it ain't rained, he's probably ready to plow."

"That's a good idea," Luke answered. "We'll take our plow, and that'll make the job go faster. Breakin' a new field is hard work. I just don't like to leave Sarah here alone. Don't guess I'll ever be easy as long as there's still Indians around."

"I'll fetch Lucas and tell him that we are going to Adam's place. I know he would want to hunt along the way. Maybe Lucas and I could go though the forest and scare up some small animals so we will have something to eat when we get there."

"Good idea, Nathan, I know Adam won't have any food ready if we just show up."

"Please, Pa, can I go, too?" Sarah asked. "It ain't far, and I can help by picking out the root pieces after the plow. I just baked a Johnnycake that I can take. I can cook on his fire same as I can on ours. I ain't been off this place for a long while. I'd really like to go . . . please, Pa."

"You'll need to get out the buckskins you wore in the Indian village. It's rough walkin' over there," Nathan said, as though it were settled that she were going.

"Do I have to wear them? Sarah protested, "I never wanted to see them again after I wore them to clean all the ashes out of the burned cabin. I got so dirty then."

"If you are goin' with us you do. We ain't stoppin' every other step to get your dress loose from the briars." Pa overrode her objections.

"If Adam's going to live over there with his sister, maybe you'd think about clearing a path wide enough to walk through, so's I could wear my regular clothes. Maybe she and I could go back and forth and visit. It sure would be nice to see a woman again instead of looking at nothing but men all the time and, worse, listening to you. All you talk about is hunting and fishing and crops and Indians and . . ."

"Sarah!" Luke's voice warned her, "If you don't want to hear men's talk, you can stay here today. No doubt Adam will want to talk about the same things as we do. I don't want you to be sorry you didn't stay home to clean house."

"Sorry, Pa." Sarah hung her head, holding back the tears.

"Sarah, if we walk back and forth often enough there will be a path," Lucas said quietly.

Sarah was surprised at Lucas's kind remark. She knew she had gone too far. It wasn't often that Pa used that tone of voice on her. She knew she'd hurt his feelings. It wasn't his fault that there weren't any women for Sarah to be friends with. She'd try to make up for her burst of temper.

Quickly, she changed into the hated buckskins. She was surprised at how soft the skins felt on her body. She had much more freedom of movement in them than she had in her cumbersome skirt. Maybe they weren't so bad after all. To keep her hair from getting tangled in the branches, she braided it and tied it with a thong. It stayed neat when done that way.

She gathered up the freshly baked bread and packed it into a pouch. She added a cake of lye soap she had made and a gourd made into a dipper. She wondered if she should take a chunk of salt. She discarded that idea when she remembered that Adam had brought her the salt when he visited the lick. He's sure to have brought some back for himself. She did add a packet of herbs for seasoning. Men didn't pay much attention to how things tasted—when they cooked for themselves—as long as their hunger was satisfied.

"Come on, Sarah," Lucas called, "If we're goin' to help Adam, we need to get there before he gets the work all done."

Sarah walked outside, wearing her tan buckskins. The sun reflected off her golden hair. She drew glances from Luke, Nathan and Lucas.

Luke suddenly realized that Sarah was no longer a child but had become a beautiful young woman. He hadn't noticed her when she wore her faded homespun dress. But now she stood before him as proud and lovely as a blond Indian princess.

CHAPTER SIX

GETTING CROWDED

"What a good day we had at Adam's yesterday. Can we do it again soon, Pa?" Sarah asked as she stirred the mush for breakfast. "I'm so glad that Delia is going to be able to stay with us. If she's as nice to be with as Adam, I'm going to hate to see her leave when Adam has their cabin ready. At least she'll be close enough that we can visit."

"My, how you go on, girl. There's too much to do in order to stay alive to worry about doin' much visitin'," Luke answered. "We need to get your garden planted today. Remember, we'll have another mouth to feed. Like as not, Adam will be here as often as his work allows, too."

"That's good. He makes me laugh. He's not an old sobersides—like Nathan. I really like the music he played on his flute. Lucas has learned a song from him already. I wish I could get Lucas a real flute like Adam's, though he does real well on the reed flute that Nathan made for him. Did you see Lucas's face when he heard the sounds that Adam's flute made? I think he liked the flute almost as much as he likes honey." Sarah enthused as she stirred.

"Sarah, ain't that mush stirred enough? Don't know which is going faster, your spoon or your tongue. I ain't never heard you talk so much in the morning. You jabber worse than the blue jay that followed us though the woods," Nathan said.

Nathan, being younger than Sarah, always had a chip on his shoulder. He hadn't liked being called a 'sobersides'. Besides, he and Lucas had formed an alliance and had plenty to laugh at that Sarah didn't know about.

Mostly, Nathan and Lucas laughed when they could get by without washing. It became a game with them to try to outsmart Sarah. When they were off hunting together, they plotted against her and found things to laugh about. Sarah didn't have the same sense of humor. Neither did Pa. He was always working, and Sarah was always cleaning. Nathan was glad to have Lucas as a brother and a friend who had the same carefree attitude that he had. They had developed a deep kinship.

Nathan and Lucas had many serious discussions. They planned that when they got the claim the way Pa wanted and were a little older, they would head west. It was getting crowded around here. As much as they liked Adam, they could see the smoke from his chimney. Adam was settling a couple of miles from them, and that was too close. Lucas had the wanderlust more than Nathan.

"Nathan, there are more families moving into this area. Soon we will have neighbors within walking distance all around us," Lucas said.

"I know, Lucas. Before Adam made his claim, it was a good day's walk to the settlement, and at least another day to Sam'l's place."

"I remember the Shawnee talking about the big river to the west. They said it was so big and wide and dangerous that just a few had tried to cross it. I wonder how far that river is from here."

"I don't know, maybe a couple of days' walk. I wonder how old we would have to be, Lucas, before Pa would let us go and explore. I wouldn't mind getting away from here and from Sarah for a while."

"Game is plentiful here, but I remember hearing that some of the Indians who had braved the river crossing came back and told of great herds of buffalo. I would really like to hunt buffalo. One buffalo would feed a family for a long time, and the hides are big and thick"

"I'm dreaming that someday we will set out west and see what is out there. I don't know of anyone who has gone west and has come back. I wonder if Sam'l would take us with him if he goes west."

"Lucas, now you have hit on a good idea. All we have to do is convince Sam'l to go west, and we can go along."

CHAPTER SEVEN

THE TRADERS

"**B**oys! We need powder and lead for the rifle before the snow falls. You did well huntin' this year, so we have a good sized bundle of skins to trade. I'm pretty busy here, and I thought maybe you two could go to the fort without me. The Indians have been quiet, and you both are careful in the woods. What do you think about goin' on your own?"

"Whoopee!" Lucas jumped up and down with glee. "Nathan, we can do it. Pa, we'll be so careful. You'll be proud of us."

Nathan, wanting to show how mature he was, strove to be more reserved than Lucas, even though his heart was pounding with excitement. "Pa, can you spare us the rifle, or should we just take hunting spears? We'll carry some jerky. There's water a'plenty on the way, so we won't need to carry water skins. We can snare game to eat. We can leave at daybreak."

"Nathan, I know I can trust you to be careful, but livin' out here, there are things you don't know about. Not all men are honest like Sam'l and Adam and the men you know at the fort. Last time Sam'l was here, he told me about some trappers who were not our kind of people. Seems there have been reports from settlers headed in to trade who've been robbed of their pack of skins by these supposed trappers. You know the ways of the woods, but men like that can be much more dangerous."

"We'll be careful, Pa," both boys assured him.

Neither of them slept well. They were too excited about their proposed adventure. They were pleased to be so trusted by Pa, although Sarah had hovered over them, peppering them with advice and concern.

♔

At the first hint of daylight, they were preparing to leave. Each carried a tightly rolled pack of skins neatly tied with thongs. Sarah had packed a parcel of cornbread and jerky. Picking up their blanket rolls, they were ready to go.

"Take the rifle, son, but try not to shoot anythin'. Use your snares and huntin' sticks for food if you can. You won't need to shoot anythin' big. It would be wasteful. You couldn't carry it along with what you already have. You should have enough skins to get lead for shot. The lead will be heavy, so you may want to take turns carryin' it back. We'll have plenty of time to hunt when you get home. Make a good trade, but be fair in your dealings. Maybe, if you have any money left and there's flour at the fort, you could get a small bag of it for Sarah. Just be careful on the trail."

Excited, they set off toward the fort. They walked for several hours in silence, each wrapped in his own thoughts. Nathan was aware of his being responsible for Lucas. Although Lucas was a good woodsman, he was still a child and apt to be a bit careless when he felt he was in a safe environment.

"I hear something in trouble," Lucas said. "It's over there." He gestured toward a tangle of trees.

"Be careful, we'll go see. You go on that side and I'll go on this," Nathan responded. "It could be a bear, from the sound of it."

Cautiously, they worked their way through the thicket toward the sound. Whatever it was making the racket was thrashing about and struggling.

"Drat these vines. I'm caught here good and tight." The voice came from the mass of trees.

"It's a man," called Lucas. "He's caught good and tight and he can't get loose."

Both boys now came together where the stranger was trapped. "What happened, mister? How did you get in this fix?" Asked Nathan.

"I was just going along, and I slipped down that bluff into this mess. I set the whole pile loose on me when I fell. My leg got wedged. I can't move that tree branch, and I thought I was a goner before you came by. Get me out of here."

"We'll get you free. Your leg don't appear to be broke, just stuck."

Carefully, they wedged another limb under the fallen log that was holding him captive. The logs seemed to have been washed down a creek bed in a flood, and it would take only a slight nudge to unbalance them. Fortunately, it was not the rainy season, so there was no danger of a flash flood.

"You can probably pull your leg out now," Nathan grunted, straining to lift the log. "Just don't pull on any of the other branches around you. Back straight out."

Silently, the man extracted himself and got to his feet. "Mighty obliged to you, men" he flattered them. "I'd have been buzzard bait for sure without your help." He brushed stray twigs from his clothing and picked up his fallen rifle.

"Where you headed?" he questioned them.

"To the fort to get powder and lead for shot," Lucas announced, innocently. "We got skins to trade."

"Well, we ain't going to get there today. Getting you loose took a long time, so we'll just camp for the night and get there in the morning." Nathan was not pleased that Lucas had blurted out his information about the skins.

"I'll just join you, if you don't mind. I've got some coffee in my pack."

"That's fine. Lucas, why don't you see if you can get a rabbit or squirrel, and I'll make a fire?"

Soon, Nathan had a brisk blaze going, while the stranger brought up wood for it.

"I'm Nathan, and my brother, as you know, is Lucas. If we're going to share a meal we should know who we're with."

"Name's Silas." Nathan noticed that Silas seemed to have only one name, and he didn't offer to shake hands. There was something about him that made Nathan uneasy. He didn't volunteer his last name, and he didn't meet Nathan's eyes when he talked to him. It was as though his mind was on something else while he worked.

✂

It was dark by the time they finished eating, and soon they rolled into their blankets around the fire and prepared to sleep.

Uncomfortable, Nathan rolled over to get to a better position. Something caused him to open his eyes. He roused enough to realize that there was only one other sleeping mound by the fire.

Quickly, he crawled over to where Lucas slept. Putting his hand over his mouth, he wakened him.

"Lucas, Silas is gone and so are our pelts. He tricked us—and after we helped him to escape!"

"What can we do, Nathan? Pa trusted us with those skins. We need shot for the winter hunting. He'll never trust us again."

"We're going to get them back. We need to get to the fort and warn them there's a thief out here, but first we get the skins."

"Let's go now. It's almost light enough to see if he left a trail. He ain't very careful in the woods, so he may be easy to follow."

It didn't take them long to find a trail, and soon they caught up with Silas who had thought he could outrun the youngsters. He had underestimated them, and carrying two packs had slowed his progress—but he was too greedy to abandon one.

"Lucas, stay back, I'm going to get our stuff. He thought we were too easy, but I'll show him." Nathan circled around until Silas came into view. Nathan rushed headlong into him, knocking him to the ground. Silas pulled a knife from his belt, and they began to grapple on the ground. Much larger and stronger than Nathan, and a street fighter, Silas had the advantage. He pinned Nathan to the ground and was about to cut his throat when a shot rang out. Silas grabbed his arm and let go of Nathan. Nathan was bleeding from several knife wounds. As Lucas ran up, trying to reload, Silas ran off into the woods, holding his wounded arm and dragging his rifle. Lucas was more concerned about helping Nathan than he was about catching Silas.

Nathan's wounds were painful but not serious, and after they had been treated and wrapped with plantain leaves, both boys gathered up the packs of skins and headed for the fort. There they would get help to catch the thief.

In a couple of hours, they reached the fort and told their stories to others, some of whom had also been tricked and lost their furs. Nathan's wounds were attended by Martha, and they turned over their packs to James.

James asked, "Can you find his trail? We don't need his kind in these parts, and he probably is headed to where he has more stolen furs stashed."

"I think so. He has a ball in his arm where Lucas shot him. That should slow him down some. I owe Lucas my life."

"Well, let's go get him and teach him a lesson he won't forget." Matthew said.

They went back to where the fight had taken place, and with no difficulty they were able to follow the felon's trail. They found him bathing his arm in a stream in front of a small cave that held several packs of skins. Coward that he was, he begged for mercy.

James said, "I'm goin' to cut that ball out of your arm so you don't lose it."

"I would like to skin him alive and let the ants eat him for trying to kill my brother," Lucas said.

Nathan secretly wished he could wrestle Silas, but Matthew made the final judgment. He always made wise decisions. "We are almost at the river. We'll build a raft, set him on it without oars and set him loose on the river. We'll keep his weapons so he can't hurt anyone again. Maybe somebody will see him floating down the river and rescue him, but not until after he has had the fear of God put into him. If nobody finds him, so be it."

Swiftly, they accomplished the mission, and soon Silas was just a dot on the water, floating slowly downstream.

"If he sees any of his friends, they'll know not to come around these parts to do their thievin'. Nathan, you earned his rifle by getting the skins back, and Lucas, you should have his knife for saving Nathan. No telling how many people have lost a year's worth of skins to him."

"Thank you, Matthew," Nathan said, knowing that the decision was right and that he had earned the rifle. The thing that worried him was how he was going to explain to Pa that he had been careless and had been tricked into losing the skins. He also wondered how he could repay Lucas for saving his life. He owed him forever.

At that very moment, Lucas was deep in thought. The next time he saw Silas, he vowed, he would use the knife on him.

CHAPTER EIGHT

A PLEASANT MEETING

"This is Delia," beamed Adam as he entered the cabin. "Delia, meet Luke, the man who helped me find the best place in the whole world to make a claim. And this young lady is Sarah. She can teach you whatever there is to know about living in the wilderness. Where are the boys?"

"Welcome, Delia, we are glad to see you." Luke said.

"Welcome, Delia. I hope your journey was a pleasant one. We are glad to see you." Sarah said with a slight curtsy.

"I am happy to finally be here. The trip was long, but I was willing to go through whatever it took to come to be with Adam," Delia answered sweetly.

"I hope that you won't mind being crowded up like we are. I know it ain't . . . isn't what you're used to, but we'll try to give you as much comfort as we can," apologized Sarah.

"Oh, Sarah, don't worry about me. I am just glad to finally get here."

The cabin was spotless. Sarah had scrubbed every visible surface and had threatened the boys with dire hunger if they came inside before Delia arrived.

"The boys have gone fishing so's they wouldn't make a mess. Miss Delia, you'll be meeting Lucas, who probably is your nephew. I don't feel that we tricked Henry, but we didn't do anything to change his mind once he denounced Lucas."

"I know, Luke. Adam told me about it."

"It's been on my conscience ever since that day. Adam knew he was a Peabody, and he used to have a crooked leg, and . . ."

"Luke," interrupted Adam, "Delia knows how much Lucas wanted to stay with you. Living with the Indians as he had, he would never be happy in Boston. Especially at Henry's house."

Delia finished Adam's thought. "I don't even feel comfortable in that house. His wife is even more particular about manners and dress than Henry. Lucas would have been miserable."

"I appreciate your understanding. Lucas is a delightful child," Luke said.

"I am sure he is. Why don't we just let things stay as they are for a while? After all, I am going to stay here in the same house with him. Maybe I can understand his needs during that time."

Luke was grateful for the ease with which Delia had handled a difficult situation, and he was more than willing to let the issue rest. Moreover, he felt that Delia was going to be a good friend for Sarah.

"I suppose understanding Lucas could take some doin'," Luke said.

"Adam told me that he had been taken by the Indians when he was very young. I feel for the boy, as he never knew his real parents and thought he was an Indian."

"When we got him he was a passel of problems. It took the better part of a year to get him to feel comfortable in this family. We were about to give up on him a number of times. He took to Nathan, and those two became blood brothers. I remember the first time he called me 'Pa'."

"I feel that Lucas is in the best place possible."

"I thank you for that, Adam. Sometimes he and Sarah get into a fray about his cleanliness. But that ain't new. Nathan needs reminding, as well.

"Luke, why don't we go see if we can help the boys catch some fish and leave the women to get acquainted? Sarah probably wants to hear woman talk for a change."

"Good idea, Adam." The two men left the cabin, relieved to be outside in the open air. Neither of them was comfortable inside when the weather was nice.

Inside, Delia looked around the cabin. She saw that the rafters were hung with strings of dried beans and onions. Cooking utensils hung on pegs near the fireplace. The trestle table was set with wooden spoons and bowls ready to hold the savory stew that simmered in the pot on a tripod over a small fire.

"Oh, Sarah, this cabin looks so homey."

"I am glad you are pleased, Delia."

Sarah nodded toward the bed in the corner and said. "This will be your bed, Delia, the boys and Pa will sleep across the dogtrot in the other room. That will give us some privacy until breakfast."

"What a beautiful quilt on the bed."

"That was my Gramma's. It was her memory quilt. Since she died I have been putting my memories on it."

"Yes, Adam told me your Gramma died during the Indian raid. I'm so sorry."

"I thank you, Delia. I miss her and mamma a lot."

"I've been admiring this fireplace. It is the biggest fireplace I've ever seen. It is strong and sturdy and dominates this part of the cabin. It makes one feel safe."

"Yes, it does. It's been through the burning of the cabin. In fact, it's all that was left when Pa came back from the hunt and Nathan and I was took."

"Nathan and I were taken," Delia unconsciously corrected Sarah. "I'm so sorry—I didn't mean to correct you. It's just that in Boston I taught school, and correcting grammar has been a bad habit with me. I'm working hard on not doing that, but like right now, I slip every once in a while." Delia blushed with embarrassment.

"A teacher? You're a teacher!" Sarah squealed in excitement. "Will you teach me? I want to learn so many things. Pa's so tired after a day's work that I don't like to bother him. I can read letters, but it takes me a long time. Nathan can read. He says girls don't need to clutter their minds, so he won't help me. Lucas doesn't want to learn. He says all he needs to read is sign for game and tracking. Oh, please, please teach me," Sarah begged.

"Of course I will!" Delia laughed. "I wish my students in Boston had your enthusiasm. I brought some books with me."

"Books?" Sarah cried. "Books. Where are they? Oh, I can't wait."

"They're in the trunk that a man named Sam'l is bringing over when he gets back into the settlement."

"Sam'l? Sam'l our family friend. I'm glad he's bringing them."

"I'll tell you what we'll do. You teach me how to cook game and I'll teach you to read and write. You see, I can cook a little—like you can read a little. We're starting out even," Delia answered.

They smiled at each other. Then, spontaneously they hugged, sealing the friendship. Sarah's heart sang. She knew ahead of time that Delia's coming was going to be a good thing. She just hadn't realized how wonderful it would be.

CHAPTER NINE

THE LESSONS BEGIN

"That stew was delicious, Sarah. Next time you make it, I would like to help." Delia leaned back from the table with a satisfied sigh.

"The next time we have stew, you can make it. You can teach me how to write the recipe for you. You can make stew as good as this or better from what Adam hunts for you," Sarah said. "The taste changes from the meat you put in it, so you have to change the seasonings. You'll soon learn.

"Nathan, Lucas, after we clean up, Delia's going to teach me to read better. It won't hurt either one of you to sit with us and get some learning, too."

"Sorry, Sarah, I can't," replied Nathan. I set some traps in the woods. There's been a wolf after Nibbles. I know you'd rather have a dead wolf than a dead sheep, so I'm going to check my traps. Besides, wolf skin will come in handy this winter." Thus, Nathan escaped from the lesson.

"I have to help my brother," Lucas said.

"No, Lucas," Luke stopped him. "Nathan can read, and you're goin' to learn. This ain't goin' to be a wilderness forever. You need all the skills you can learn."

Reluctantly, Lucas watched Nathan quickly slip out of the door before Luke changed his mind. Lucas would obey. He would do whatever Pa told him. He owed him his life.

As was his cautious way, he would watch Delia before he made up his mind about her. Already she had made a good impression on him. She didn't hug him when they met. In fact, she scarcely seemed to take notice of him. He liked it that way.

As they sat before the fire with an old Boston newspaper that Delia had wrapped in her bundle, Lucas studied this woman who was supposed to be his aunt. He was still trying to comprehend the relationship. Like Sarah, she smelled good. When she touched his hand while pointing to a word in the paper, her hand was soft. Sarah's hands were rough and callused from hard work. The fabric of her skirt was different, too. He decided that it had a city-feel, so he tried not to let it brush against him. There were things about her that he liked and things that made him uncomfortable.

Sarah got up from her stool to place another log on the fire. Spring nights were still chilly. She wanted Delia to be comfortable.

"Sarah, you move so silently. My shoes clatter on the floor. How do you do it?" Delia asked.

Puzzled, Sarah thought a minute. "Oh! It must be my moccasins. All of us wear them. There's no place to get shoes out here, and moccasins are easy to make and wear. All you need is a well-cured hide."

"Will you help me make a pair? They certainly look comfortable," Delia asked.

"Of course. I've put back some skins in the loft. Tomorrow I'll get them down and we'll make you a pair. You won't want to wear shoes again," Sarah answered.

"That's good, because this pair of shoes is almost worn out from walking from the settlement. I asked the cobbler who made them back East to construct them strong enough for the wilderness. He assured me that he had, but evidently the wilderness is stronger than the boots that he makes."

"We walk everywhere out here. It sure is hard on shoes, but moccasins seem to fare better. We'll get started on yours tomorrow when I can see what I'm looking for up in the loft," Sarah assured Delia. "Once you wear them, you'll wonder how you could walk in those shoes."

As the girls talked, Lucas began to sidle toward the door, hoping to get away from the dreaded lessons. It was not to be. From the corner of her eye, Delia saw his movement and stopped him.

"Lucas, let's finish your lesson. Come over here to the fire. Please get a piece of that charred wood to write with. Here's a nice flat piece of wood for you to write upon. Now, let's start with the letter 'A'. An 'A' is a teepee with a bar across the middle," Delia explained.

Maybe this wouldn't be as bad as he expected, Lucas thought. He'd wait and see. He had already learned that it wasn't going to be easy to escape from the lessons or from the woman who saw everything.

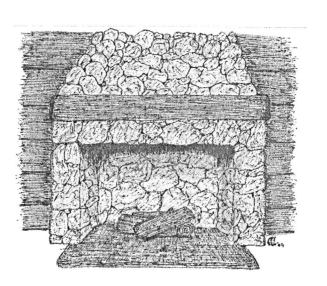

CHAPTER TEN

DELIA GOES NATIVE

"The wild strawberries are about ready to pick. A couple of days ago, I saw some white ones turning pink up on the ridge behind where the blackberries grow," Nathan announced.

"And I suppose you want me to pick them for you," Sarah responded.

"Well, yes. And you'd better wear your skins to get through those blackberry bushes. They'll tear you to pieces. Stickers on 'em seem to be meaner than usual this year."

"And would you like to help us pick the strawberries?" Sarah teased.

"I would, but I have other work that I have to do."

Sarah knew that Nathan would find the first sweet things growing anywhere around them before anyone else did. He and Lucas were constantly alert for anything that would satisfy their sweet tooth needs.

"Wear your skins? Delia puzzled. "What are you talking about?"

"Deerskins that I wore in the Indian village. I ain't grown much since then, and they still fit me. Now, I wear them when I go into rough places in the woods. The saw-briars and branches tear my dress. I ain't got time or cloth to sew a new dress, so I wear my skins, like Pa and the boys do."

"Are they like the boy's skins?" Delia asked.

"Almost, except mine has a skirt instead of britches. They really feel good, and they keep the thorns from scratching. They get hot in the summer, though," Sarah explained.

"May I see them?" Delia asked. "They sound like something I need to make so that I can help Adam in the woods. I don't plan to be a burden to him, so whatever I can find that will make it easier for me to be of aid to him will be useful. I'm trying to learn as quickly as I can."

"I know you are, Delia. But, like me learning reading, it will take some time."

Sarah brought out the Indian dress. It was brown and as smooth as she could scrape the skins before she laced them together into a shirt and skirt. The design was practical and simple, but the outfit protected her from the scratches, and the skin wouldn't tear easily. Delia held it in front of herself. "It'll surely take more skins to make one for me than it did for you. I'm a lot bigger than you are. Where we going to get enough? She questioned.

"Pa brought in a couple of bucks that we dressed out last fall, but we didn't have time to cure the skins for clothes. We didn't need them at that time, so we just put them in the loft to work up later. If we soak them in the creek, they'll soften up enough so we can scrape them easier," Sarah explained.

"I don't believe I should go in the woods and look for strawberries wearing these clothes," Delia observed.

"No, Delia, I'll take the skins to the water to soak. Then tomorrow, when I go for berries, you can start scraping. We can put them with some skins that are already cured and make you some skins to fit you for going out in the woods. I wish there were some quills or beads to make a fancy outfit for you, but there ain't, so we'll do a plain one. Some of the Indian wives had outfits that were really beautiful. They wore them at the feasts."

Lucas listened quietly and made a plan.

CHAPTER ELEVEN

BEARING GIFTS

Sarah and Delia, both wearing deerskins, emerged from the brush thicket. Their arms were filled with lengths of white oak.

"Sarah, I'm almost breathless. I haven't worked this hard for a long while, if ever."

"I know, Delia, sometimes I forget that I've been out here for a long while, and I don't know any other life than work on the frontier."

Sarah was teaching Delia how to split oak to make baskets for the new cabin Adam was building. Adam was now in the process of cutting and squaring logs with which to build it. The baskets would be used for storing and carrying things that they would use.

When Adam had the logs ready, Pa, Nathan and Lucas would help him raise the cabin, just as Sam'l had helped them. Cabin raising was a job that required help.

While the girls were gone, Sam'l had arrived on one of his unexpected but always welcome visits. This time, he pulled a travois on which he had loaded Delia's small trunk and a bundle. He and Luke had learned from Lucas how to make the dragging rack to haul things. It was also one of the many skills of the Indians that the settlers had adopted for their own use. The forests were so thick that horses and wagons were unable to get through them to the outlying cabins. As usual, Sam'l brought a surprise.

"I sure am glad that Lucas knew about this totin' rig," Sam'l gestured toward the crossed poles which he had pulled behind him. "This little trunk weighs as much as if it were full of rocks."

Suddenly, Sam'l eyes widened as he caught sight of the two girls walking toward the cabin. They looked like Indian maidens. Surely, this tall, graceful girl wearing Indian dress was not the prim and proper Boston woman he was expecting to see. She wore her clothes with ease and moved as though accustomed to the rough terrain. This must be Adam's sister, he thought.

"Hello Sam'l, it's good to see you again," Sarah said. "Delia, this is Sam'l. He is the best friend a body could ever have. He's helped us get settled, and he's always bringing things to make life easier, and . . ."

"Easy, Sarah," Sam'l said. "I'm just doin' for you what you'd for me."

"Sam'l, we don't do near enough for you."

"You keep me fed good when I can't stomach my own cookin' any more. Miss Delia, I am right glad to meet you."

"We're grateful to you, Sam'l," said Luke. "Delia has learned a lot in the short while she's been here. She sure has taken to the wilderness. You'd never know that she came from city folks."

"Now I'm getting embarrassed," Delia said. "The trunk is full of books. That's why it was so heavy. I couldn't bear to leave them, so I left my good clothes instead. I didn't think I was going to any tea parties out here."

"I don't reckon you will," laughed Sarah. "The only tea we have to drink is sassafras tea, and you don't want to drink too much of it or you'll get a stomach ache. I been thinkin' I could maybe brew some herbs together that would taste good. If you have a hankering for tea, I'll see what I can find," she offered.

"That sounds good. I really like the warmth of tea, but I don't enjoy the small talk and gossip. I had to endure a lot of that at the tea parties in Boston."

"Living in the wilderness doesn't lend itself to gossip, Delia. We are more concerned with survival."

"I know, and I can really begin to appreciate the severity of life out here. I can only imagine what life is like in the winter."

Sam'l interrupted. "Well, I didn't bring tea, but I did bring somethin' you'll like." He took a bundle from the travois. "Here, Luke, best you handle these."

Luke opened the bundle and found four small trees wrapped in damp moss and leaves.

"Sam'l, we got trees all around us, more trees than we need—so I'm guessin' these trees must be special."

"They are. Feller named Johnny came through a couple of years ago. He kept a sack of apples with him, and every time he ate one, he saved the seeds. Then he planted them wherever he thought they would grow. He planted some up in that clearing above my cabin. These trees were healthy lookin' and got a good start, so I dug 'em up. You need to plant 'em where they get sun, this Johnny feller said. I still have two growin' there. If they bear like he said, the apples would just go to waste with me. You got more stomachs to fill here."

"Was he called Johnny Appleseed?" Delia asked.

"That's him," Sam'l answered.

"People were talking about him in Ohio when we came through. They laughed about him and said he seemed a bit touched in the head about apple trees."

"Pa, we can have fried apples, and dried apples, and I can cook some with honey. Oh, Sam'l, thank you! You did it again, you brought the best gift ever." Sarah was excited about the trees and what they would bear.

"You're much obliged, Sarah."

"Well, let's plant the trees before we start pickin' the apples." Luke smiled at Sarah.

"Pa, can we share two of the trees with Adam and Delia and plant them over at their place?"

"Good idea, Sarah."

Lucas listened and wondered if apples were sweet. He'd be sure to watch them so nothing hurt the trees.

CHAPTER TWELVE

A CHANGE

"**M**iss Delia, roastin' that meat the way you did sure did make it tasty." Sam'l sopped up the juices with his cornbread and wiped his chin with the back of his hand.

"She's learning real fast," Sarah complimented. "She can make moccasins and baskets and birch buckets. She's learned to skin rabbits and squirrels, and . . ."

Delia interrupted, "Sarah, Sarah, Sarah, I'm just learning whatever I can that you teach me. If it weren't for your help, I wouldn't be able to do these things at all,".

Sarah smiled and looked down. "I'm mighty proud of you, Delia. You have done wonders in a short time."

"Guess Adam's about ready to start puttin' up the cabin." Luke tried to change the subject. "He should have the logs trimmed and ready to move to the place where he wants the cabin to be built."

"I'll be goin' his way tomorrow," Sam'l said, "should be some turkeys roostin' on that knoll I'll pass to get there. I ain't et turkey in a while."

"Oh, Sam'l, if you shoot a turkey, please save the wings and the big feathers for me. They make the best dusters," Sarah pleaded.

"If I get a turkey, I'll not only save the feathers, I'll ask you to clean and cook the bird."

"I'll gladly clean the bird. But Delia can cook it. She knows a way I never heard of. She says that in Boston, they stuff them and bake them. She cooked some ducks that way that Nathan brought in. I never tasted anything as good," Sarah said.

"Stuffed them with what?" A confused Sam'l asked.

"Well, cornbread and onions and seasonings. The juice from the bird flavors all of it and makes it moist. It's quite tasty," Delia explained.

Nathan and Lucas exchanged glances.

"What's wrong with Sam'l? He ain't talked so much with anyone except Pa," Nathan observed.

Lucas nodded. "He never stayed as long as he does now, nor has he ever come back so often."

"How we going to get Sam'l alone to talk about going West." Nathan wondered.

"I don't know, but we got to get to him soon."

The boys were not the only ones who noticed a change in Sam'l. He himself wondered what was happening to him. He was actually enjoying talking to a woman. Usually, he avoided being around them. Sarah didn't count. He would always think of her as a little girl. He hadn't trusted a woman since Becka. Then everything changed for him. He shook himself. This was not something that he wanted to think about.

"It's still early. I believe I'll head for Adam's place tonight." Sam'l felt that he had to get away.

"Sam'l, it's late enough that you would be arrivin' after dark. Especially if you shoot a turkey," Luke said.

"I know Luke, but I've walked in the woods at night before." Sam'l felt that he had to get away. He didn't like the feelings that were beginning to stir in him. He didn't understand why he felt so easy in Delia's presence, yet at the same time so uneasy. All those desires he had buried with the memory of Becka. He had to leave, but he didn't want to. Maybe the silence of the forest would help him sort out his confused feelings.

CHAPTER THIRTEEN

SAM'L'S DILEMMA

Since Adam's cabin had been completed and Delia had gone there to keep house for him, Sarah was often lonely for her company. Even though they lived fairly close, both of them were too busy to see each other very often. Also, it was not safe for either of them to travel through the woods alone. The men were too busy to leave their place for a full day unless it was to help each other.

Since Sam'l did only what was necessary to keep his claim, he was not so fettered. He came more and more often to Luke's place, stopping only long enough to eat a meal and spend the night. As always, he never came empty-handed. Sarah now had wooden trenchers he had made for her to serve as plates. He brought game that he had shot or trapped close by and skins that he had cured. Sometimes he arrived with a brace of birds in each hand or a string of freshly caught fish.

From Luke's place, he went to Adam's to help him get settled, just as he had helped Luke. He carried gifts to Adam's, as well. Often, Sarah sent something to Delia that she thought she could use.

In turn, when Sam'l returned from Adam's, he brought news of Delia to Sarah and sometimes a book for Sarah to read. Most of the news dealt with how well Delia was coping with the difficulties of living in the wilderness. He said to Sarah, "Delia has braided a mat of wild vines to lay in front of the hearth."

"I am glad, Sam'l, that she is doing so well."

"Also, Sarah, she gathered wild flowers before the frost and tied them in bunches to hang with the beans and onions from the rafters. They really look pretty and they make the room smell good. Delia made a basket of twisted grape vine that held the nuts she had gathered. And she is helping me with my way of talking so I am more careful and I am also learning how to read better. All thanks to Delia," Sam'l said.

Sarah cringed. All Sam'l talked about was Delia. In fact, every time he came over he talked about the Blakes—especially about Delia Blake. Sarah blushed at her own anger. What was the matter with her?

✄

One day, Sam'l came slowly through the woods and watched until he saw that Luke was alone. Softly, he whistled to attract Luke's attention. Realizing that Sam'l didn't want to be seen, Luke signaled him to meet at the creek.

"Hello, Sam'l, what brings you to our parts today?"

"Oh, Luke, I don't know what I am going to do," Sam'l said.

"Are you in some kind of trouble?"

"Well, not trouble exactly, except in my own mind."

Luke was suspicious as to where Sam'l was going with his remarks but decided to play dumb. "I don't rightly know what you are talking about, Sam'l"

"Oh, Luke. I don't know what I'm goin' to do," Sam'l moaned. My head is so mixed up. All I can think about is Delia. She's everything a man could want, but I'm scared, Luke, I'm real scared. I need advice. Will you help me?"

"I'll try, Sam'l, but I can't promise I'll do any good. Why don't you start from the beginnin' and tell me why you're scared."

"It's hard Luke, I've buried all the memories so deep and for so long that I ain't sure I can bring them out, but I'll try."

"I find, Sam'l, that bringin' out old memories can help."

Sam'l started to unload his burden. "There was this girl back home. No, I don't mean this home out here, I mean back east. She was beautiful, smart and fun to be with, and she was my girl. I thought we shared so many good times. I told her about my dream to come out here and make a home. Her name is Becka. She told me she loved me, would wait for me, and go anywhere with me. I left to stake my claim.

"Were you gone a long time?"

"I was gone a year. I came out here and staked a claim, and I planted a crop."

"Year's a long time, Sam'l."

"I know it is, Luke, but when I went back she was still waitin' for me. I told her about the frontier. I didn't hold back. I told her about all of it, the good and the bad. Then I went back and raised the crop and built the cabin, sort of a rough cabin. Then I went back to get Becka." Sam'l shoulders sagged.

"What happened next, Sam'l?"

"When I went back to get Becka, she was gone. She said she loved me, but she married a lawyer in Philadelphia. Her mother told me that she didn't want to worry about Indians and primitive living conditions. She needed friends around her. I was broke up."

"I can understand how you would feel about Becka, Sam'l."

"I was so upset that I blamed myself. I could have stayed at home and been a merchant like my father. But no, I had to go and find my own life. None of my family understood my feelings."

"Sam'l, life is a compromise. I don't know how else to put it. You know of my losses. I still don't know what to think sometimes."

Sam'l continued, "When I lost Becka, I lost all desire to live, but something drove me on. Then, I met you and together we got Nathan and Sarah back from the Indians. I saw your love for them and how that love made you keep tryin' to rebuild here in the wilderness. I came to love them, too. They are my family."

"Those are good thoughts, Sam'l."

"But now I'm thinkin' about Delia like I thought about Becka. I'm afraid, Luke. I can't go through that kind of hurt again. What am I goin' to do? I don't want to live without Delia, but I'm afraid to ask her to live with me as my wife." Sam'l was shaking with emotion as he finished. He rubbed his sleeve across his eyes.

Luke kept his eyes on the stirring spoon he was whittling. He wouldn't embarrass Sam'l by taking notice of his emotions. Finally he said, "Sam'l, Delia ain't Becka."

Luke was caught up in his own memories. He remembered how Lizabeth had died of a fever. He still missed her and often cried at night for her loss. He was more fortunate than Sam'l as he had Nathan, Sarah and now Lucas. He would think carefully about what he should say to Sam'l, as each person has to live his own life.

"Luke, I feel a little better havin' talked. I don't know what to do yet, but I'll think on your words."

CHAPTER FOURTEEN

JUST TALKING

"Nathan, let's go fishing. We're caught up with the chores, and if we stay here at the cabin Pa will have us clearing another field, or Sarah will be fussing about tracking in dirt."

"Sure, we'll get a mess of fish for her to fuss over."

The two boys sat on a flat rock at the creek. It was a lazy summer day. Birds were serenading each other in the forest. A lizard sunned itself on an adjacent rock, and in the woods behind them a woodpecker carved his presence in the tree. A butterfly flitted over a clump of wildflowers at the edge of the water. The boys' corncob bobbers floated on the slow-moving water, waiting for a fish to snap up the bait they trailed just under the surface.

Nathan stretched his arms above his head and yawned. "It's a plumb lazy day," he drawled.

"Wonder what it's like over by the big river? Do you think it looks like it does around here?" mused Lucas.

"I don't know, but I don't think it is very civilized. Adam told me about it after he went looking for a place to settle. He said it was more wild than it is around here. I sure would like to see it for myself."

"Me, too. I want to go somewhere where there aren't so many people. These days, you see someone living every five miles. It's getting too crowded for me."

"I feel the same way. You can't go anywhere without seeing a new cabin on a new claim. Maybe we could find a place nobody's ever been before."

"Maybe we could find my tribe. You know, the one I lived with when I was growing up. I know they were planning on moving farther west—too many white men coming in here."

"Lucas, you talk about going back to your tribe. Do you wish you had never been rescued and raised as a white boy? Would you still want to go back to being an Indian? Do you miss living like that?"

"I don't know. It's been a long time. There's good and bad. I liked hunting and fishing and learning to become a brave. Best of all, I didn't have to worry about wiping my feet before I went into a teepee, and nobody was fussing about me being clean all the time."

"And what's the other part?"

"I like being with you and Pa and—sometimes—with Sarah. Especially when she makes me corn cakes and strawberry jam. Pa is a good man. I would miss him if I went back to live with the

Indians. I don't know how the tribe would feel about me now. I probably have too many ways of the white man for them."

"But you are a white man."

"Maybe I don't have a choice any more. But what I really want is to see the buffalo so thick you can walk from one side of the herd to the other on their backs."

"Maybe we could catch a young one and train him to pull the plow. It sure would be easier than pushing it though new ground," Nathan dreamed.

"I wish we maybe could get Sam'l to go with us. I s'pose he could catch us one. He knows all about how to trap animals without hurting them. And we could use his strength to help us dress out the ones we kill for food. I hear those buffalo are pretty big."

"Oh, Lucas, you don't trap buffalo, you shoot 'em. Besides, Sam'l's got other things to do with his time. He's getting married," Nathan worried. "That sure will spoil all our good times."

"Well, maybe Adam might want to go."

"I don't think so. We could ask him, but he seems satisfied with his place here. He likes breaking in a new field and making a homestead for himself. He used to be willing to try new things, but he's getting old and wants a permanent place."

"No harm in asking."

"No, I guess not. Maybe we will have to wait a while. I don't think Pa would let us go alone. When we become men, we can do whatever we want."

"I can't go against Pa's wishes, Nathan. He saved my life twice and I owe him."

CHAPTER FIFTEEN

A CHANGED SAM'L

"Pa have you noticed how Sam'l is changing lately? I do believe he's washed his buckskins," Sarah commented as she strung beans to dry.

"I've noticed. He's sure been comin' a whole lot more, though he don't stay as long. Last time he came, I asked him if he wanted to go with me to flush out that covey of quail I saw behind the ridge. He said he didn't have time. He had to go to the Blakes'. He had some logs seasoning over there that were ready to work up. He promised to make Delia a bench with a back on it,"

Nathan commented with disdain, "Used to be, he'd jump at the chance to get to the birds. What's wrong with him?"

"He acts funny, too," Lucas added, "Last time he was here he just sat on a log and didn't do nothin' but stare at a tree and mumble under his breath. If he was with the Indians, they'd probably think he was off his head and act like his spirit had left him."

Lucas and Nathan were concerned about Sam'l. They had not had the opportunity to ask him if they all could go to the big river, maybe cross it and hunt buffalo. Sam'l's change in behavior was upsetting to them.

"You all just treat him normal-like. He ain't crazy, as Lucas suggested. He's just trying to sort some things out," Luke counseled.

"What kind of things?" alarmed Nathan asked.

"Ya, Pa, what's Sam'l got to sort out?" Lucas asked.

"Well, it's personal stuff with him."

"Does it have to do with Adam and Delia," Nathan pursued.

"I think I've said enough for now," Luke said with some finality.

"Pa, do you think I can go to see Delia next time Sam'l comes?" Sarah asked. "I ain't seen her in such a long time. I've got some gourds dried for her and some seeds I've saved. Sam'l can see me through the woods. Can you get along without me for a few days? I'm caught up on the drying and stringing for a while. The way Sam'l's been coming so often, he'll be here soon."

"Who do you think should do the cookin' while you are gone?" Luke asked.

"Nathan or Lucas. It would do both of them good if they was to cook and then clean up afterward."

"If I cook, I'll roast game outside on a fire and there won't be any cleaning up afterward. Right, Lucas?"

"That's right. If Sarah leaves for a few days, I won't go into the cabin and I won't get it dirty. Then it won't need cleaning," Lucas rationalized.

"You two boys are right smart at avoidin' work. Well, Sarah, if Sam'l is willin' to see to you, it's all right with me. But you know that we are goin' to walk on your clean floor," Luke said.

"Oh, Pa, I never even thought about what kind of mess I might find when I get home," worried Sarah. "But I feel it in my bones that I need to see Delia."

ꙮ

"Hello, the cabin," Sam'l called. "Anybody home?"

"Come in, there's beans cookin' in the pot," Luke said.

"I brought a chunk of boar I killed and smoked. Can you use it, Sarah?" Sam'l asked. "I brought a piece for Delia, too. Thought I'd go over there first thing in the mornin'."

Sarah felt some jealousy. She wasn't sure why. Nevertheless, she asked Sam'l, "Oh, Sam'l, thank you for the meat. Will you take me with you to visit Delia? It's been so long, and Pa said it's alright with him, and I won't be any trouble to you, and she . . ."

"Sarah! Sarah!" Luke stopped her. Let the man get into the house before you start plaguin' him with your wants."

"I don't know, Sarah. Do you trust your clean house to three men?"

"Oh, Sam'l, don't tease me. I dread what I'll come back to, but I really want to see Delia."

"If it's not against what your Pa wants, yes, I'll take you. Reckon Delia is as hungry for woman talk as you are. Besides, there's somethin' I want to see her about. It might be handy to have you there with me."

Luke and Sam'l exchanged glances. Luke was relieved that he wouldn't be asked for advice.

Nathan and Lucas exchanged glances, as well. But it was different for the boys. They shared a certain sense of disappointment; they felt their dream was slipping away.

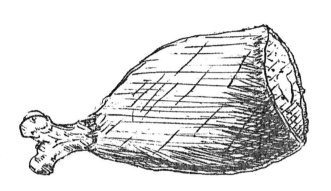

CHAPTER SIXTEEN

DELIA'S DECISION

Tossing and turning on her bed, Delia wrestled with a problem. She had come to the Kentucky wilderness to make a home for Adam, her beloved brother. Now she was torn between her wish to move on and her guilt about leaving Adam on his own.

Unable to sleep, she finally gave up the attempt and rose from her tumbled bed to poke the fire.

"I'll just finish stringing those onions I pulled yesterday. Might as well do something rather than waste good working time," she decided.

She braided the almost-dry stems of the onions to make a string of them to hang from the rafters.

As her fingers flew during the braiding, her mind flew even faster.

"I just know that he doesn't eat right. He has to be lonely in that cabin all by himself. His buckskins could use a good scrubbing. I imagine his cabin is pretty bare. Oh, why can't I stop thinking about Sam'l?" She worried.

Adam had wakened when she got up, but, sensing that she needed to be alone, he lay on his bed pretending to be asleep. Something was bothering his sister, and when she was ready she would share her feelings with him. From the time they were babies, they had a special relationship with each other. He was attuned to her distress.

Only two years separated their births, and when their mother died they drew closer in their loss. Both Henry, their older half brother, and Lucas's father were much older than they were. Either Adam or Delia would begin a sentence and the other would finish it. A look of understanding would flash between them, or they would laugh at a shared joke while other observers would wonder at what was so funny. Most of all, they shared a love for this wonderful land to which they had come to make a home.

Now Adam felt as though a wall had come between them, and he silently worried.

Delia was pondering her choices. What was the right thing to do? She and Sam'l had become good friends. More than friends. She knew Sam'l wanted to marry her. She was uncertain as to where her loyalties were. Was she to become Sam'l's wife, or was she to keep house for her brother.

For several days, Delia went silently about her tasks. No longer did she sing as she worked; her brow remained slightly furrowed.

Sam'l and Sarah arrived about noon. The noon meal hadn't been eaten yet, so they became instant guests. Adam liked Sam'l. He knew that Sam'l liked him, but he was suspicious that Sam'l wasn't coming to see him. So Adam and Sarah went outside, leaving Delia and Sam'l in the cabin alone.

"Have you talked to Adam, Delia?" asked Sam'l.

"No, I haven't, not yet."

"But you do want to become my wife, don't you?"

"Yes, Sam'l, I really do, but I don't know how to tell Adam."

"Do you want me to tell him?"

"No, Sam'l, that is something I must do."

The pair lapsed into silence as Adam and Sarah returned to the cabin. Adam sensed an uneasy silence but didn't know why.

Delia finally said to Adam, "We must talk soon. I have something to tell you."

Unusually clueless, Adam wondered as he worked just what Delia would tell him. She seemed to be in good health.

ℬ

Several days later, Sam'l got ready to escort Sarah back to her home. It had been a delightful visit for all of them.

"Delia, I really enjoyed our visit. It is always so good to see you even though I don't see you often enough," Sarah said.

"I appreciate your visit as well, Sarah. I am sure that Adam enjoyed visiting with Sam'l."

Adam interjected, "I did enjoy both Sam'l and Sarah." He smiled at Sarah.

"We best be on our way, Sarah, I do thank both of you for your hospitality," Sam'l said.

With their goodbyes over, Sam'l and Sarah left Adam's place and disappeared into the lush forest.

That evening, Adam and Delia sat before the fire—Delia knitting and Adam writing in his journal as he did every day. Eventually, Delia raised her eyes and watched Adam put away his writing materials. He cleaned the quill with which he had been writing and carefully closed his ink well. Then, settling back with a sigh, he folded his hands across his stomach and waited for her to speak.

"Adam, you know how much I love you and this beautiful place to which we have come."

"Yes, Delia, I know."

Delia hesitated. "Adam, I find myself wanting more."

"Like what, Delia, what do you want? Maybe I can get it."

"Not likely, Adam. I would like to have my very own family, a husband and children and a claim of our own to work."

Adam's jaw dropped. "Did I hear you correctly, you want to get married?"

"Yes, Adam. I do. I want that for you, too. I want you to bring home a wife and have children. It's time for us to move on with our lives."

"Oh, Lord," Adam uttered. "I wasn't expecting that. I reckon I should have, as much as Sam'l has been here. It is Sam'l, isn't it?"

"Yes, Adam, it's Sam'l. I do want to marry him, and he wants to marry me. We know it won't be easy. Especially leaving you, Adam. That will be the hardest part of all. I don't rightly know how I will do it." Delia hung her head and started sobbing.

"Delia, you are my sister. I understand your needs. We will always be close. We have shared life for over twenty years. But I agree, now it is time to move on. I like Sam'l but, admittedly, I've never thought of him as a brother-in-law."

Reassured, she continued, "Lately, I have been thinking of how kind and thoughtful Sam'l is. I know he is a bit rough around the edges, but his heart is huge and filled with love. I just have been torn between the two of you."

"There is no reason to be torn, Delia. Sam'l is a good, honest man. I know that I can trust him to be a good husband to you. I want you to have a wonderful life and be happy. When the time comes, I know that you will want the same for me."

"Adam, you are the best brother in the whole world. The next time Sam'l comes over, will you tell him that your sister would be happy to be his wife?"

"That I will gladly do for you."

CHAPTER SEVENTEEN

A WEDDING IN THE OFFING

"Pa! Pa! We got news for you." Luke looked up from where he was working at the woodpile to see Sarah and Sam'l coming into the clearing. He paused, stood upright, and mopped his brow.

"Pa, Delia and Sam'l are getting married. They want to get married here at our cabin, where they met."

Just then, Lucas and Nathan arrived on the scene. "What's all the racket, Sarah? You sound like a screech owl," Nathan said.

"Sam'l and Delia are getting married. Delia is coming over here to use my spinning wheel to make a mattress cover. I told her I had some flax she can have. It's retted and beaten and ready to use. There's so much to do, and Sam'l said we only had a month. He said he's waited for her all his life. He ain't waiting any longer. I've got to start cleaning up this place, and you boys have got to help me. It's a mess!" Sarah grabbed a broom and started sweeping the floor.

Lucas and Nathan faded back into the forest.

Sam'l leaned against the door frame and grinned foolishly. "She's right, Luke. I'm ready to jump over the broom with Delia.

Don't know as I deserve her, but I'm goin' to do my best to make her a good husband."

Luke took Sam'l hand. "Sam'l, you deserve Delia. You'll do just fine as a husband."

Sarah interrupted, "Sam'l, do you remember all that you have to do at your cabin? I wish I had time to go over there and clean before Delia gets there. I'll make out a list for you so you don't forget anything."

Luke shook his head and said, "Oh, Sarah."

There was no way Sam'l wanted Sarah to see his cabin as it was now. It was truly a cabin inhabited by a single man. He had piles of half-cured, smelly skins stacked in the corners, and the dirt floor was covered with wood shavings and dried bones that had fallen on it. His few pieces of clothing were tossed wherever he had taken them off, and his working tools were scattered about. Since he was the only one living there, it hadn't mattered to him before. Now, though, he had much to do before he brought his bride into his home. Marrying certainly would change his way of living. He supposed he should put in a floor of boards and maybe hang a skin over the one window that was cut in the wall. Before, he had just pegged up a piece of wood to keep out the critters.

Sam'l thought of everything he had to do and broke into a sweat. "Luke, I can't stop with you this trip. Between Delia and Sarah, I've got enough to do for three men." Sam'l prepared to go on.

"Sam'l, you ain't going without eating!" Sarah bustled.

"Yes, Sarah, I am. I got one month left to decide when and what to do, and eatin' is one of those decisions. After that, I'll gladly let my wife decide, but until then, I'm livin' like I'm used to. I'll be here next month for the handfastin', one month from today." Sam'l said firmly.

"Sam'l, sit down and eat this plate of beans and a piece of cornbread," Sarah said and put the plate on the table.

Luke said, "Relax, Sam'l, eatin' a plate of beans won't delay you too much."

Nathan asked, "Do you need an extra hand, Sam'l? I kind of got used to the peace and quiet when Sarah was gone. Lucas can help Pa with what we have to do, and I can help you. I guess you'll have to put a floor in first thing, and I can help with that."

Sitting down to the plate of beans, Sam'l said, "That's neighborly of you, Nathan. If your Pa can spare you, I'd appreciate the help."

"There ain't nothin' here to do right now that we can't do without Nathan's help for a while. He's been itchin' to get away, and now he has a reason," Luke responded.

"He'd just get in our way and make a mess when Delia and I are trying to get ready for the wedding," Sarah added. "We're going to have to clean everything in here. Pa, where can I find the best pine branches? Or I guess I could use cedar if you have to go too far for the pine. I need some cut to hang in the lofts so it smells good in here."

"Now, Sarah, we're just goin' to jump over the broom. Then, when the circuit-ridin' preacher gets here next year, he can say the proper words over us. It ain't goin' to be no fancy ceremony, but we'll be married as fast and true as we'd be in a big church back East," Sam'l protested.

Sarah could be as stubborn as Sam'l. "A girl just gets married once. It's going to be as nice as I can make it, even though we're the only ones here, and it ain't going to be fancy. We'll even have music. Adam can bring his flute, and he and Lucas can play. Oh, I wish we had some people to come."

"We'll have all the people we need," Luke said. "It don't take but two to make a marriage."

The room fell into an uneasy silence. Then Lucas asked a question. "I don't understand about jumping over a broom. What is that for?"

"Lucas, I don't rightly know how it got started, but jumpin' over a broom is like crossin' from one life into another, from single to married."

"Seems like white man's foolishness," Lucas said somberly.

"You *are* white, Lucas," Sarah said.

"I know, but I don't understand everything about being white."

Lucas and Nathan headed out the door, as they had to make some plans about what to do about Sam'l. He was their only answer for an early trip to the big river.

CHAPTER EIGHTEEN

A TRIP TO THE FORT

"Pa, Sam'l said that Delia needs to go to the fort. She wants Martha to teach her how to build her own loom."

"Can't you show her, Sarah? You made yours."

"No, Sam'l said Martha learned a new way to set the warp threads from a lady who was passing through on her way west with her husband. I'd kind of like to go, too, and learn a better way to weave. I was wondering if maybe you could take us. Adam can't go right now, and the boys can take care of our place. Oh, please, Pa, it would be so good to see those people who were so helpful to us."

Luke understood Sarah's desire to see people she felt an obligation to. He also knew that since they had returned after she had been captured, except for a short visit to Adam's, she had not been off the homestead. It had been lonely for her.

"Let me study on it, daughter. We'll see." Luke was trying to plan his chores so that he could take the girls. He knew that it would take them at least a day to walk there and another to walk back. Maybe it would take even longer; that would depend on how well the girls could keep up with him. He wondered how much they planned to carry. That could slow them down. He realized that they would be carrying more on the way back. He expected them to want to stay long enough to learn everything that Martha had to teach. It appeared to involve at least a week, perhaps more. He worried about leaving Lucas with Adam that long, but he knew that Sarah deserved to go.

The next morning, as Sarah prepared breakfast, Luke said, "Sarah, if you want to go to the fort, I'll take you and Delia next week. I'm goin' to Adam's in a day or two, and I'll bring Delia back here with me. We'll leave from here. We can't be gone long, and I don't want to lose good workin' time."

"Oh, Pa," she jumped up and ran to him. She threw her arms around his neck and hugged him. "I'll have to clean the cabin before we leave."

She grabbed her broom and began sweeping the already clean floor. "If Delia is coming here, I don't want her to come to a dirty house."

Delia arrived at Luke's place wearing her buckskin outfit. She carried a small poke that contained the few things she would need for the trip to the fort.

"I'll wear my skins, too, Delia. We can move faster if we aren't worried about briars and such catching on our clothes. We'll leave early in the morning, if you're not too tired."

"That's fine. I'll be ready at sun-up."

Sarah prepared a package of food to take along. "Now, Lucas, I've made you and Adam food to eat, but mostly you'll have to care for yourselves. I'm leaving the cabin clean, and I expect to find it that way when I get back. Please don't track in mud and dirt. Wash your hands before you eat. Don't make a mess when you cook. And . . ."

"Sarah, we won't even go inside if that will make you happy. We can cook outside and sleep in the lean-to if it rains. We ain't goin' to mess up your precious cabin," protested Lucas, who was insulted by her lack of faith in him and Nathan to care for things.

"You know you never pay attention, you just track and scatter. You don't mean to be messy, but you are."

"Sarah, if you are goin' to worry about keepin' the floor clean, maybe you'd rather stay home and clean. I'll take Delia to the fort alone so you can fuss about the messes," Luke interrupted.

"Oh, Pa, I just get carried away sometimes. I'll stop worrying."

⚸

Early the next morning, the three of them set out for the fort. In some places they had to walk single file, and in a few other places they could walk three abreast. Luke usually led the way, with Sarah following him and Delia bringing up the rear. They stopped to eat their lunch by a beautiful, tranquil stream and quenched their thirst by scooping up the clear water with their hands. After a short rest, Luke picked up his rifle and stood, ready to continue.

"I got stiff sitting there so long, Pa. Guess I need to walk more places," Sarah teased.

They were within sight of the fort when Delia stumbled and fell. "Stop a minute, please. I seem to have turned my ankle. I can't put any weight on it," she said with tears in her eyes. "Oh, why wasn't I more careful? I didn't notice that root in the path."

Luke examined the ankle. "It don't appear to be broke. Lean on me, Delia. Can you hobble as far as Martha's?"

"I think so; it's not that far now."

Martha had seen them coming and ran out to help. "Oh, you poor dear. Let's get you inside and soak that ankle before it swells too much. I don't believe it's broke, but you'll have to stay off of it," she sympathized.

"What a mess I've made of your outing, Sarah."

"No you haven't, Delia. We can still learn about the loom. That's what we came for."

"You girls will stay here and we'll get you ready to build your own looms. The woman who showed me the new way came from England. Her mother worked in a mill that made cloth. Seems they worked from daylight to past dark in a place that had no heat in the winter, and it was so hot in the summer that they couldn't breathe. They were poorly paid and sometimes beaten across their backs if they didn't work fast enough. She and her husband wanted a better life than working in the mills for their children, so they indentured themselves to a merchant and came to the colonies. After their indenture was up, they decided to come out west and make a claim. The sad part about it is that they never had children," Martha informed them.

"Martha, I'll cut you some wood." Luke wanted to escape her chatter. She was a good woman, but it seemed her tongue was never still. "After I cut the wood, I'm goin' over to the general store and check into the bunk house behind the store. I need to catch up on what's happenin' at the fort."

He cut and stacked the wood and then ambled over to Matthew's cabin. He was about to open the door when it was flung open and he was knocked down by a furious young man who barreled out of the cabin.

"Don't you ever come back," screamed an angry young female voice from inside. "Who do you think you are? You keep your hands and mouth to yourself. I wish I had a log in my hands when I hit you. Now, git!"

"Whew! What happened? Can I help you?" Luke got up and dusted off his clothes. "Who was that sorry-looking young man you just threw out?"

Matthew's daughter, Ruth, was flustered. Her face was red and she glowered, with arms akimbo, as she sputtered, "He tried to kiss me! I hope I knocked some teeth loose when I slapped his face. The very nerve of him! He treats everybody like they should fall down and worship him."

"Well, he's gone now. Who is he?" questioned Luke.

"Who he is isn't as bad as who he thinks he is. His name is Helmut von Schlecht, but he thinks he is a fine lord or something. He is a bully, and I would trust him as far as I can throw that old oak tree. He is so stuck on himself, nobody can stand him. The sad thing is that his mother is really nice, but she can't see anything wrong with him. She's a widow and he's her only chick. You might remember her. They came here about the time you left to go back to the cabin. Her name is Frau von Schlecht," explained the outraged girl.

"Think I do remember her. She seemed nice enough but kind of shy. Didn't know she was still here."

"Yes, both of them are. He's talkin' about goin' farther west, but I think she'd like to stay here. He wants to go, so she'll likely do whatever her spoiled son wants. He knows he's not welcomed anywhere around here. It's his own fault—him and his high and mighty ways! He can't go soon enough for me. He'll come to a bad end!" Ruth predicted.

"He can't be that bad! What the boy needs is a lot of hard work. You're just upset, Ruth. You'll feel better when you calm down. Now, where's your Pa?"

"He should be in the field with James. He'll be glad to see you—and I won't ever feel better about Helmut von Schlecht."

Since Ruth was a large girl, she was capable of doing damage to anyone who threatened her. From what Luke saw of the von Schlecht boy, he was not as large a person. He was slightly built and had a pallid complexion. Luke didn't get a good look at his face, but he saw something mean in the young man's eyes. He would wait and see for himself what kind of man Traudel von Schlecht had reared. He remembered her and decided to pay her a visit soon.

CHAPTER NINETEEN

GUESTS

"Pa, Frau von Schlecht has been very kind to us. This morning she brought a cake that she called 'kuchen'. I think she is anxious about going on west. Her son is not happy at the fort. Delia and I have been so busy with Martha's loom that we haven't had time to meet him yet. He didn't come with her when she visited. She did ask about you and said she remembered how kind you were to her when we were in the fort after the raid. She is a very nice lady."

"Yes, Sarah, she is very nice. I am not so sure about her son. I've been visitin' around here, and, so far, people have avoided talkin' about him. I guess if they can't say anything nice, they figure it's best if they don't say anything at all. Maybe it's because he is different from the usual settler."

"What do you mean, Pa?"

"Well, he's more stiff and formal than they're used to around here. He also expects that people will do what he says. I understand his father was some kind of aristocrat back in Germany. That's what the 'von' is for."

"Well, he ain't in Germany now. Where's his Pa?"

"I don't know. Frau von Schlecht never talks about herself or her family. People don't pry out here. Everyone's past is his own business."

"I guess in some cases, we're better off not knowing, but I'm sure that Frau von Schlecht's past is as innocent as yours and mine," commented Delia.

"I guess I'm a little curious about her, but I don't really want to meet her son," Sarah said.

"Luke, my ankle is so much better, I think we can leave to go home in another day or so. Martha wrapped it and James made me a walking stick. If we go a bit slower I can keep up. The rest helped me more than anything. Martha wouldn't let me put my foot on the floor. If we don't leave soon I'll be so fat and lazy that I won't be able to walk."

"That's good, Delia. I've left Adam and Lucas with my chores long enough. Let's be ready to go early; we will leave when the sun is up."

Luke left to say his farewells, and while he was gone the girls had a visitor. It was Frau von Schlecht, who had a request.

Shyly, she asked, "Please, can my son and I go with you as far as your cabin? Then we would go on toward the big river to seek a new future in the great wilderness."

Sarah said, "I'm sure Pa would welcome you to travel with us and to stay at our cabin until you are ready to leave."

"I am most grateful, Sarah. My son, Helmut, is anxious to leave. I am concerned about the safety of traveling westward."

"Frau von Schlecht, feel free to travel with us and spend a few days at our cabin before heading west."

"I thank you, Sarah," Frau von Schlecht said, and then she left.

છ

Luke returned a little later, and the girls told him of the plan. "I wish we had time to talk about this before you offered," he said cautiously. "She is a good woman, but I'm not sure about Helmut. From what I heard around the fort, I feel that he won't get along with either Adam or Lucas".

"Sorry, Pa, but it would be only for a few days."

"I reckon we'll see, won't we?" Pa answered.

℘

Early the next morning, at sun-up, they were ready to leave. They waited for the arrival of Frau von Schlecht and her son. Luke was beginning to pace in front of the cabin when Frau Von Schlecht arrived, breathless.

"I'm so sorry to be so late. Helmut is not feeling well this morning. He told me to go on without him and he would follow when he has recovered from his malaise. He said he would just slow us down today because he felt too weak to maintain the pace you would want to set. I don't know what to do."

"Traudel, your son is old enough to fend for himself. You can come with us and he can follow later," Luke said.

Sarah's eyebrows shot upward when she heard her father address Frau von Schlecht by her first name.

Luke continued, "When he feels better, James can give him directions to the cabin, and besides, there is a trail for him to follow."

Luke was relieved at not having to put up with Helmut. He was happy that the trip went smoothly and that Frau von Schlecht did her share of carrying and helping with the cooking as they paused for rests and for overnight. She was a pleasure to have along, clearly very gracious and kind.

℘

87

When they reached the cabin, Frau von Schlecht said, "Oh, it is just beautiful here. The gourds at the door make your home feel so welcoming. And these young men must be your brothers. Guten Tag, Nathan and Lucas."

"Hello, Frau von Schlecht," Lucas said. "This is Adam, Delia's brother. My brother Nathan's not here right now; he's gone to help Sam'l fix up his cabin for when he get married."

"What a good job you have done keeping everything so clean while your father and sister were gone, Lucas. My, that rabbit you are cooking smells delicious."

"Adam got it with his sling. If we knowed you were coming along, we'd have better meat. We didn't know you were coming today, Pa. I don't know if we made enough food for all of us." Lucas was embarrassed at the attention.

"Don't worry, Lucas, it won't take a minute to make more," assured Sarah.

"I brought some 'Kartoffel' from the fort. I'll be happy to prepare them if Sarah will allow me to use the skillet."

"What's 'Kartoffel'?" whispered Lucas to Adam. "She sure talks funny."

"I don't know. We'll just have to wait and see when it's cooked. If we don't like it, we can pretend to eat it and give it to the dog."

Seeing their confusion, Frau von Schlecht enlightened them, "Oh, pardon me. Sometimes I forget the word in your language. 'Kartoffel' in German is potato."

When the potatoes, steamed with onions and bits of smoked pork, were served, everyone showed their appreciation by their appetites.

"Pa," Lucas whispered, "Frau von Schlecht is a great cook. I'm glad you brought her along."

"I didn't exactly bring her. She came on her own and she is waiting for her son to meet her here, then they are going west. He should be here tomorrow."

"I remember him from the fort," noted Lucas. "Can't say that I like him very much. He is a bully. He may try to push us around."

∅

It was a week before Helmut von Schlecht made his grand appearance. His mother was worried that his illness had developed into something serious, and she considered returning to the fort to care for him.

"What do you have to eat?" were his first words to his mother.

"Oh, Helmut, my Liebchen. I was so concerned that you had met with some misfortune. I was going to ask Luke to permit someone to escort me to the fort to care for you."

"Mutti, you forget that I am a man who is very capable of caring for himself. It was foolish for you to worry about me. Now, I am fatigued. Where am I to sleep?"

Lucas shrugged and silently slipped outside, joining Adam at the woodpile, where he was stacking logs. Lucas had developed an instant dislike for Helmut, the son of Frau von Schlecht.

"I don't like Helmut at all, Adam. I don't trust him."

"I don't like him either, Lucas."

"He can't be that nice lady's son. Who does he think he is? He didn't say he was sorry for being a week late."

At that moment, Helmut came out of the cabin. "I am Count Helmut von Schlecht. You will show me where I am to sleep."

Lucas asked, "Count? What's a count?"

"Count is my title. It shows respect. You must call me count. Call me Count von Schlecht."

Helmut turned on his heel and went back into the cabin. Lucas just stared after him for a few seconds. Then he started to grin. "We have to sleep in the same cabin with him. We can make sure that he don't get too comfortable. I'll fix his bed for him. I'll gather some of these burrs from the woods and put them under his covers."

"Maybe we can talk Sarah into brewing some sarsaparilla tea for him," said Adam. "That would give him a good bellyache. He would be running to the woods all night."

"And when he goes, we can point him to a patch of poison ivy. And how about putting a snake in those fancy boots he's wearing?" Lucas added.

"I can't let on that I know anything about it or Pa will take a birch rod to me," he thought to himself. Then, aloud, he said to Adam, "Tomorrow I'll take him to the creek, to the slippery rock, the one with the slimy moss all over it. If he accidently falls in . . ." His voice trailed off for a moment. Then, quietly, almost to himself, he muttered, "He'll sure to stay long enough for us to show him how much fun we can have here." Lucas chuckled as he planned his revenge.

✄

It didn't take long for Helmut to get ready to leave. Craftily, he was planning to go on alone. His mother could care for herself, and she wouldn't be trying to tell him what do if he were alone. He figured that she had sold all of the family jewels she had brought with her from Europe, so there wasn't any reason for him to stay with her. This was a good place to leave her and, who knows, it might come in handy for him some day. Sarah wasn't at all bad looking for a girl of her class.

Late the night of the second day, he stealthily rose from his bed and, carrying his boots, he crept from the cabin. Lucas, awakened by the motion in the room, watched Helmut through slitted eyes as he took only his own rifle and gear. Had he tried to steal anything else, Lucas was prepared to fight him.

"Good riddance!" Lucas whispered to himself after Helmut had departed. "I wonder if he's gone to tell his mother goodbye or to get her to go with him? No, he wouldn't be slipping out like he is. He's goin' to leave her. She'll be better off without him. I hope he don't wake Pa, 'cause Pa might try to stop him." Entertaining these and other thoughts, Lucas fell back to sleep once more.

In the morning, Lucas carried to the cabin a note to his mother that Helmut had left behind. It was short, and she read it aloud. "I have gone to seek my fortune alone. Don't try to follow me. I will be better off alone. Count Helmut von Schlecht."

"Oh, my!" exclaimed Frau von Schlecht as she folded the note.

Luke was angry. "He didn't even think about how his mother would feel. He was just thinking about himself."

Sarah said, "She will be better off without him. It is better that he's gone on alone. What a toad he is! How could such a nice lady have him for a son?"

"What will Frau von Schlecht do now?" Lucas asked.

✗

"I had a visit with Frau von Schlecht, and she feels that she should go back to the fort. She doesn't want to be a burden to us out here," Luke said.

"She's no bother, Pa," Sarah said.

"Well, I know, but she'd be better off in the fort than she would be tryin' to find her worthless son. Like a bad penny, he'll probably return."

"Yes, I am sure he will be back when he needs her help again," Sarah said.

"She told me that her husband was a mean man and raised Helmut as he saw fit. He would not brook interference from her in his discipline and was harsh with her. One day she had enough, so she bundled Helmut up and ran away. She took all the jewels that her mother had left her, went to Hamburg and bought passage on a boat to New York. She was seasick on the trip and spent most of the voyage in her cabin, while Helmut made friends with a crew of rough seamen. After they landed, Helmut and his mother joined a wagon train heading for the wilderness, and the train took them as far as the fort. That's where we met them. She was glad to get away from her abusive husband. But now she is distraught and wants to go back to the fort, so I will take her." Luke completed the longest speech he had ever made.

The next morning, Sarah and Lucas said their goodbyes to Frau von Schlecht, who cried as she and Luke started for the fort.

Several days later, Luke returned from the fort. He seemed subdues, unusually thoughtful and quiet. Nobody dared to ask him why, but they all suspected something.

CHAPTER TWENTY

THE CEREMONY

"It's almost time for Sam'l to come back, and I still haven't got the cabin ready for the wedding," mourned Sarah.

Delia had spent several weeks with Sarah. She had woven a mattress cover, and she and Sarah had fashioned the dress that she was to wear on her wedding day.

Nathan had returned a few days ago to report that Sam'l's cabin was ready with a new floor—and very clean. They had even built a lean-to outside, where he could store all of his pelts. Nathan had called Lucas aside and reported that Sam'l had declined their offer to lead them to the West. "He seems smitten with Delia."

Lucas responded. "I was a'feared of that."

"Maybe that should be a lesson to us if we ever think of getting married," observed Nathan.

Lucas slowly shook his head. "I don't understand why Sam'l had to get married. Wasn't he happy before?"

"I don't rightly know that either, Lucas." Sarah started talking again. "I'm going to need some pine branches tomorrow. I'm going to hang them all around the walls and put some berries in them. Then I'll need to cook the wedding dinner, so you go get me whatever you can find to eat in the woods, Lucas, and I'll add garden vegetables that I am going to use. Nathan, you get the ham from the smoke house and enough hickory cut and split so that I can cook it slow over the fire outside."

"Sarah," Nathan spoke sharply, "This ain't your wedding." Then he blushed as he realized that his anger was not at Sarah.

"Pa, can you think up enough jobs for the boys to do so they keep out of the cabin and keep it clean? Maybe we can have some fish with the ham. The boys could go fishing. I want this to be a wedding that Delia will be proud of, something she can tell her children about when she gets older."

"Daughter, slow down. You're gettin' way ahead of yourself. Don't you think Delia might want to have something to say about the wedding?"

"She and I talked about it, Pa. It's going to be nicer than what she said she wants. It's my surprise for her and Sam'l."

"I know you think a lot of both of them, Sarah, but . . ."

At that very moment, Delia and Adam arrived at the cabin. Sarah swept the floor one last time and fluttered about, straightening benches and the table.

"Welcome," Luke said to Adam and Delia. "Looks like this is the big day for you, Delia."

Delia blushed. "I am mighty pleased that you are letting us use your cabin for our wedding. It means a lot to Sam'l and me."

"You look mighty pretty, Delia," Sarah added.

"Sam'l's not here yet, Luke?" asked Adam.

"Not yet, but he will be."

At last, Sam'l appeared. He was dressed in a new pair of buckskins that he had made. His hair was combed, after a fashion, and he smelled clean. His face beamed with joy as he stepped into the cabin.

They were all crowded into the cabin. "Why can't we just go outside where we'll have some room to breathe?" Lucas asked.

"That's a good idea. I feel like I'm smotherin' in here," Sam'l groaned.

"It ain't from bein' closed in; you're just a nervous groom," laughed Luke.

"Well, where's the broom, can we get started?" Sam'l asked.

"Not until we have some music. Adam, play something wedding for us," directed Sarah.

Adam played beautifully. Delia had tears in her eyes. Sam'l blushed a bright red.

 Sarah produced a new broom that she had made from the rushes at the creek. She placed it carefully on the floor before Sam'l and Delia.

When the song was finished, Adam said, "Delia, Sam'l, I am not a preacher and don't claim to be, but I need to say some words. Delia, you're my sister, my little sister, and I've looked out for you all our lives. I imagined that when you came out here you would keep house for me forever. I don't know where I got that idea. Maybe I was just lazy. But along came Sam'l, and that disrupted my plans. I have mixed feelings about losing my sister, but I have good, strong feelings about your wedding, Sam'l. I know these aren't the right words; what I mean to say is that I wish both of you much happiness."

Tears were streaming down Delia's face. Sarah was blinking back her tears, too.

Sam'l faced Delia and asked, "Are you ready to start a married life with me?"

Delia looked at Sam'l. "Indeed I am, Sam'l, indeed I am."

They jumped over the broom, being careful not to let their feet touch it.

With a whoop, Sam'l gathered Delia in his arms and whirled her around. "You are my wife and I am so glad."

Delia hugged Sam'l and whispered, "Sam'l, I'll be a good wife to you. I really will."

This was more than Nathan could handle. "Can we eat now?" and he headed for the door. Lucas had beaten him outside.

Nathan said to Lucas, "I feel sorry for Sam'l. His free-going days are over. From now on he will have the responsibility that will dictate his actions."

"I do too, Nathan, 'cause now he won't be able to go to the big river."

Little did both boys know the amount of truth in what they thought and said.

CHAPTER TWENTY-ONE

HONEYMOON

"Oh, Sam'l, it's beautiful!" Delia exclaimed as they arrived at his cabin. It was set far enough above the river so that the spring floods didn't reach it, but close enough to the water for easy access. Large old, oak trees formed a backdrop behind the cabin. A garden plot was between the buildings and was already planted with some of the plants breaking through the soil. There were still some seeds that needed to be planted. Multi-colored leaves covered the trees and the ground beneath them, the weathered logs of the cabin stood in gray relief against them.

"This place is so idyllic that I feel at home already."

Sam'l beamed. "I'm so glad, Delia. I was afraid at first that I couldn't make my cabin homey enough for a wife. I know that you will do wonders with what I've started. Let's go in and look at the presents we were given."

Sam'l had laid a fire ready to light before he left the cabin. In their packs, they carried Delia's clothing, the mattress cover she had woven, spoons and bowls that Lucas had carved, a stirring paddle from Luke and a small birch pail filled with lye soap from Sarah.

Sam'l laughed, "Only Sarah would think of cleanliness first."

Nathan's gift of skins awaited them inside the cabin. He had caught and cured them while he worked with Sam'l.

In the month before the wedding, Sam'l and Nathan had done much to prepare for the bride. They had moved all the traps, tools and pelts into the shed behind the cabin. They filled the small space inside the log walls of the shed with Sam'l's possessions. Then they laid a wooden floor inside the cabin. This was backbreaking work, and the floor was still a bit rough. It would be warmer than the original dirt floor and much cleaner. Sam'l's few cooking utensils were set upon the hearth. Two stools and a pile of skins in the corner were all the furnishings the cabin contained. Sam'l's needs had been few. This was about to change.

As he opened the door, Sam'l said, "It ain't much, Delia, but the two of us can fix it up. A month wasn't long enough for Nathan and me to get it ready."

"Oh, Sam'l, this is our first home. We have a lifetime to do whatever we need to do to get it fixed up." Delia blinked a few times. This home was a far cry from a Boston home and scarcely compared to Luke's home.

"Sam'l, my dear, you did put in a wood floor. I know it was hard for you and Nathan. I truly am happy. Please believe that, Sam'l."

Sam'l saw the tears of happiness in Delia's eyes. He had a hard time not shedding tears himself. He lit the fire and soon had a blazing fire in the fireplace. Next, he sliced slabs of meat from the smoked ham that hung from the rafters. Delia put some acorn squash into the pile of embers she scraped to the side of the fire. She hung the iron kettle filled with water on the rod. Soon, the spicy smells of the herb tea brewing in the kettle, the odor of the wild pork sizzling on skewers, and the woodsy smell of baking squash filled the tiny cabin. While the meat was cooking, Delia spread the sleeping skins in the corner and covered them with her mattress bag. Tomorrow she planned to stuff it with leaves. Beneath it, she would lay pine boughs. They would serve until Sam had time to build a proper bed. In the spring, they would plant corn, and she could use the corn shucks for stuffing—there was so much to plan.

Sam'l was planning, too. With his hunting, fishing and the food Sarah had sent earlier with him and Nathan, they should winter well. Many nuts and roots were still in the woods. He'd teach Delia what to gather and what to avoid. Next year, he would plan better what they needed, and they would have another storage shed.

Before the snow would fall he would meet Luke at the settlement, where Luke would deliver Delia's books and the seeds to plant a garden in the spring. He was sorry that he had not thought to use the cornhusks for the mattress. He and Nathan had plowed them back into the garden. Sam'l usually threw a skin on the ground and slept on it. His life style was changing rapidly. He was trying to decide whether to build a bed first or a table. So he asked Delia.

"I reckon we should have the bed first. We can get along for a while without a table," Delia said.

"Then I'll build the bed first, and I do have the wood cut and seasoned and ready to work up."

Sam'l seemed overwhelmed. He had never needed a bed before or a table. There were many things he hadn't needed—especially a wife. He was rapidly finding out how much he had missed during all those lonely years. He hadn't realized the years were lonely until Delia came into his life. Sam'l stood up straight and grinned at Delia. She smiled back.

CHAPTER TWENTY-TWO

THE HUNT

"I didn't think Pa would ever let us go on a hunt by ourselves, Nathan."

"Neither did I, Lucas."

"Tomorrow we can get up early and head for the Licks and get a deer. You take your rifle—but for me, I'd rather have my bow and arrows."

"I wish we had more powder so I could have practiced with this gun before we left. Guess I'll just have to really pay attention and try to hit what I aim for the first time. I'm not that good yet to feel I can hit it like Pa does."

The morning dawned bright and clear. Both boys were ready by daybreak. They were excited but needed to control their emotions until they got out of hearing range of the cabin. They had sat through a lecture from a worried Luke the night before. The reminder of Silas was there, unspoken.

He had said, "Nathan, you don't point your gun at anything that you don't intend to kill for food. If you just wound the animal, you track it down and do it in so that it doesn't suffer. Never let anything die in agony because you were careless. Don't take more than you can tote back, either. You can make a travois, but remember that it is hard to pull through the woods when it's loaded. You'll start out strong but by the end of the day, you'll feel as though your arms are pulling out of their sockets. Oh, and don't forget the salt. Sarah is almost out, and we'll need it to salt down the meat for winter."

Sarah, too, had her share of advice. "Don't step in any holes and break a leg. Watch out for low-hanging limbs so you don't hit your heads. Take care that you don't get bit by bees or spiders, and watch out for snakes."

Finally, they both tuned her out and went to sleep.

✄

"We're off on our hunt, Lucas."

"I still can't believe that Pa let us go without him."

"He trusts us, but we'll have to earn the trust and not do anything dumb like we did when Silas stole our packs."

"Well, that turned out alright. You got a rifle and I got my knife out of it. And we got our skins back."

"Yes, we did. But we might not be that lucky the next time. We must be double careful this trip."

As they got farther from the cabin they were less cautious about whispering and started talking out loud.

"If we are going as far as the Licks, that's a full day's walking. We may not get a deer tonight. Besides, if we wait until morning, we can get one while he's drinking and have a better shot. Lots of them gather at the water at first day light."

"I would like to spend many nights out under the stars. We ain't been able to do that yet."

"Lucas, we'll just have to wait to do that on another trip. Pa might be worried if we stay too long, so this time we'll get our salt and meat and get back as soon as we can. We want him to trust us."

Silent at last, they moved on at a steady pace through the woods, watching for signs of game as they trotted toward the Licks. Not wanting to waste time, they stopped at mid-day to eat some jerky and cornbread that Sarah had packed for them. Washing their meal down with cool water from the stream they were following, they were soon on their way again.

At sundown, they reached the Licks and saw signs of recent animal presence there. They made camp a ways back from the area and set a squirrel to roasting on a spit over a small campfire. While they waited for it to cook, they began to talk and plan.

"Mighty nice of Sarah to pack us something to eat. She has been real nice to me since that time I broke my leg. I thought she hated me because I was another person to mess up her cabin."

"Sarah has always liked you, Lucas. Sometimes it's hard for her to show it. She gets so caught up in the cleaning and such."

"I really hated her the first day I came, when she made you and Sam'l take me to the creek and almost drown me. I thought my hide was going to come off before she thought I was clean enough to come inside. If I could have got away, I would have run."

"Where would you have run to?"

"I don't know. I know my tribe was north or toward the north, and I guess I would have gone north until I found some Indians who would keep me. I know some Shawnee and I could talk to them."

"Yes, I remember scrubbing you. You did make a fuss. Can you still speak Shawnee?"

"I don't know. It's been over a year since I did. Maybe I could if I had to."

"Nathan, when you were with the Shawnee, was it hard for you."

"It wasn't, really. I missed Pa and Gramma, but I had fun hunting with the other boys of the tribe. They treated me real nice. I thought I would be a captive forever, so I tried to learn their ways and tried to fit in as best as I could. One thing I really liked was that I didn't have to wash every time I turned around, like Sarah makes me do.

"I was so young when I was taken that I can't remember my real ma and pa. I thought I was an Indian. I never thought I'd be captured by the settlers and taken to their camp. I was scared at first, and I decided to fight back, especially Martha. She was my worst enemy. I know now that I was wrong—she was only trying to help me."

"I remember how mixed up you were, Lucas. I'm glad that you decided to stay with us instead of going to Boston with Mr. Peabody."

"I am too, Nathan. East is the wrong direction for me. We talked about striking out West to see what the frontier is like. Now that Sam'l has did himself in with marriage, we lost our guide. We'll have to find another guide or wait until we are older."

"I want to explore the west, as well. I know we lost Sam'l and the only other possibility is Adam. I wonder if Adam is interested in exploring the west to the big river," Nathan pondered.

Both boys were dreaming of the wild west when a young buck bounded in front of them. He paused and looked, then raced into the forest. Nathan didn't get his gun off his back to take a shot, and Lucas fired an arrow into the forest where the deer disappeared.

"There will be more tomorrow at the Licks. He was mighty young. I'm glad we didn't take him," Nathan said.

Lucas agreed. "Tomorrow's another day. We'll get what we're supposed to." He went to retrieve his arrow.

The next morning, Nathan decided to wait at the Licks for game while Lucas went after small trees to cut for their travois. He had to go a distance from the Licks to keep from scaring off the deer that would come to drink.

After about an hour, a large buck approached the water and began to drink. Silently, Nathan raised his rifle, took careful aim, fired off one shot and watched as the buck dropped. Success! Immediately, Nathan began the task of removing the buck's internal organs. It was hard work, and Nathan completely lost track of timed.

It was almost midday when he heard a rustling behind him. He turned to see Lucas coming back, empty-handed.

"Where's the pulling sled?"

"Back in the woods. But come with me, Nathan, and see what I found."

"What?"

"A horse."

"A what?"

"A horse."

"Where?"

"Come with me."

"Help me hang this deer up in that tree over there so it's safe until we get back. I can't get it up there alone. I was waiting for you to help me hang it so it can bleed out. I already dressed it out. The liver is cooking on that spit."

They got the deer hoisted into the branches of the tree, and Nathan followed Lucas into the forest. They walked for about a quarter of a mile, then the forest opened into a clearing. There, in the middle of the clearing, was a horse. A brown horse.

"What is that horse doing out here? I ain't seen one since the Indians took ours in that raid."

"What should we do?"

Nathan pondered the question. "Don't know. If it's someone's horse, where is he? We can't take it if it belongs to someone, but we can't leave it here either."

"How we going to catch it?" Lucas asked.

"I don't know."

"Did you ever ride a horse, Nathan?"

"Not that I can remember. We used ours to pull the plow."

"I did, twice, in the Indian village, with a buck holding me in front of him," Lucas said.

"We ain't caught him yet."

"I know."

The boys sat at the edge of the clearing. The horse continued to eat grass in the clearing, not paying any attention to the boys.

Finally, Lucas said, "I think I can get closer to him like the Indians did. It looks like he has some kind of rope around his neck."

Lucas started to walk toward the horse, expecting the sleek animal to bolt and run. He walked a few feet, then sat down. He was murmuring something to the horse that Nathan couldn't understand. Lucas sat motionless for a while, then arose and slowly walked toward the horse again. Very close now to the horse, he stopped again, remaining standing, murmured something, and waited some more. Then he slowly turned and sat down on the ground with his back to the animal. The horse looked at Lucas and snorted, taking several steps toward the boy. Then, to Nathan's surprise, Lucas turned around slowly, and the horse ambled toward the boy. Lucas just waited until it got close enough for him to reach the rope. He reached up, slowly, took hold of the rope, and gently pulled the horse toward him. The horse came willingly.

"Good boy! Good boy!" Lucas was saying as he gently stroked the horse.

"Nathan, come here—real slow. Don't spook him."

Nathan started toward the horse. He would walk several steps and then stop and then repeat the movement. Finally he got close enough to touch the animal. He stroked its back and neck.

"He's tame. He belongs to someone."

"But who? We're a long way from anyone."

"What will we do with him?"

"First off, it's a her. She's a mare."

"Well, she's tame. I bet she's been ridden. Boost me up on her, Nathan. I'll give her a try."

"What if she bucks you off?"

"Well, what if? Just hold onto the rope."

"If that's what you want, I'll give you a boost. Here, step into my hands and I'll lift you up that way."

Nathan boosted Lucas up onto the horse's back. The horse just stood, expecting some direction from the rider. Lucas just sat there, not knowing what to do. "How do I make her go?"

"I don't know. I'll just lead you." Taking the rope from Lucas, Nathan began to walk and the horse followed. There was no doubt that this animal had belonged to someone who rode it regularly. But there was no sign of anyone around.

"Do you think both of us can ride her at once?" Lucas asked.

"She looks big enough for the both of us. I'll lead her over to that fallen tree so I can climb on."

Nathan led the horse to the tree, handed the rope to Lucas and climbed on in back of him. Both boys sat on the horse, but the brown beast just stood there, awaiting instructions.

"Well, she ain't moving. You get off and lead the horse in a circle so I get a feel of riding her, Lucas."

Lucas slid to the ground, took the rope and began to walk. Nathan sat erect, surveying the area from atop the animal. He felt like . . . an Indian chief.

The horse nuzzled Lucas. "This horse really likes me! It sure is tame. Now what do we do? Should we take the horse home to Pa or let her go? Maybe she'll go back to where she came from."

"I don't know, Lucas, I know there ain't no folks living around these parts. I don't know anyone who has a horse. Could be a runaway, or could be the rider fell off and the horse wandered off, or could be it belonged to a tribe and got lost from the other horses. We should take her home and ask Pa. "If we don't, wild animals could get her."

The boys led the horse to the campsite at the Licks and packed their gear to go home. They cut down the deer and loaded it onto the travois that Lucas had made. Adding a large chunk of salt, they were ready to leave.

"Nathan, why don't we ride on the horse and let her drag the rack? We can go a lot faster than if we try to drag the rack. We can take turns riding."

"I'm going to walk and lead the horse. We don't know enough about riding to get us home. You can ride for a while and then I will." Nathan reached for the rope halter.

"Do you think Pa will be mad?" asked Lucas.

"Don't know. You never know how Pa will take something like us coming home with a horse. We went for deer, and come home with a horse."

"We got the deer, too," smiled Lucas. "He should be glad."

ℬ

When they approached home Nathan, who had been riding, slid down to the ground so that both boys walked into the clearing holding onto the rope.

Pa was outside their cabin, chopping wood. He looked at the wide-eyed boys and the horse.

"What in tarnation do you have there?"

"It's a horse, Pa. We just found her grazing in a clearing close to the Licks. There she was, all alone. Nobody was around her. We looked for signs of her owner, but it seemed she was really alone, so we figured the best thing to do was to bring her home and ask you what to do. We couldn't leave her where a mountain lion might pick up her scent and kill her."

CHAPTER TWENTY-THREE

MYSTERY SOLVED

"**B**oys, I'm goin' to see if I can find where that horse came from. Someone might be in trouble. Tell me exactly where you found her."

They described as best they could the area where the horse had been grazing. "Lucas, you had better come with me, I don't want to waste time looking in the wrong place. Sarah, we'll be back in a week. Depends on whether we can find her owners or not. I ain't goin' to lose more than a week from the work here. We'll take the horse with us. Maybe she can give us a direction to go."

With that said, Luke and Lucas set off toward the Licks, leading the animal. "She's a nice enough critter, Lucas, but horses eat more than we got to feed, and they need to be sheltered. We ain't got no oats, and the grazin' grass will be gone before long. Let's hope we can find where she belongs."

"Sorry, Pa. We brought her home 'cause we didn't know what else to do with her."

"You done right, son. I just hope her trail ain't too cold for us to follow. She belongs to somebody."

When the woods thinned enough to ride, they got on the horse and made good time to the Licks. Soon, Luke picked up the trail that the horse had made. Following the route of trampled brush and broken branches was easy for them. On the second day, they smelled wood smoke.

I think we're comin' up on somebody. Don't know what we're goin' to get into, so you stay back here with the horse while I scout this out," instructed Luke.

Cautiously, he went forward. Soon, he approached a small canvas lean-to in a clearing. He heard the murmur of voices coming from the skimpy shelter. He crept closer.

"Amanda, I'm so sorry to have gotten you in this mess. I don't know what to do. We can't go on without our horse and you bein' so sick. Maybe if that herd of wild horses hadn't come through she wouldn't have run off with them. I thought I had her tied good, but she was stronger than the rope. We should never have left home and tried this. It's all my fault. Please look at me. Tell me you forgive me. I have to take care of the little one—just don't go and die on me."

The woman stirred restlessly on the pallet where she lay. "Jacob," she moaned, "My side hurts so bad. It feels like I'm going to explode . . . no, don't touch me! Your hands hurt. I'm so hot. Water."

Helplessly, he held her head up so that she could take a sip of water.

"Is Mama going to die?" tearfully asked a frightened little girl who was at his side.

"Not if I can help it, but it doesn't look good." Absently, he patted the child trying to soothe her.

His wife was writhing in agony and he was unable to help her. Luke had heard all he needed to realize that this was not a situation that he had to fear. He decided to make his presence known. He retreated a ways from the meager tent and called out, "Anyone here?"

"Yes! Yes! Can you help us?" the distraught man stumbled into the light, a tiny girl hiding behind him.

"What's the trouble?" Luke asked.

"I don't know. Something's bad wrong with my wife. She's in terrible pain. Keeps crying that her side feels like knives are being stuck in it. She's burning with fever, and she can't keep anything down. Our horse ran off, and I can't leave Amanda and Suzanna to get help. Please help us."

"What color was your horse?"

"She was just plain brown with no distinguishing marks on her."

"Lucas, come take care of this child, she don't need to see this, and bring the horse. Tie her to a tree. We don't want her to run off again."

"Is this your animal?" Luke asked.

"It surely is! How did you find her?"

"The boys found her and brought her home, but I felt I needed to come back out here to see if I could find the owner."

"I'm really glad you did. Maybe now I can get a doctor for my wife."

"There ain't no doctor out here. Usually, Martha—back at the fort—does all the doctorin' we have. She's days away, and I don't think you can get your wife to her right now."

After kneeling by the side of the sick woman, Luke realized that she was beyond help. She was barely breathing and appeared to be suffering from the flux that attacked many people. There was no cure that he knew of. Something inside them just seemed to burst, and the person died in great pain. For her sake, he hoped it would be soon.

Luke couldn't look at the man as he said, "I don't know nothin' to do to help her. I'm sorry."

He turned away from the raw grief on the husband's face as he prepared himself for what was to come. Father and daughter knelt by the stricken woman. At sundown, she breathed her last, rasping breath. The child was too young to realize what had happened. She chattered on to Lucas about the doll her mother was going to make for her when they found a house in the new place. Lucas fed her bits of meat from a rabbit he had speared and cooked. Soon she fell asleep in his arms while Luke and Jacob prepared a final resting place for her mother.

Luke fashioned a crude cross and set it upon the cairn of rocks that were mounded over the new grave.

Jacob and Luke sat at the campfire. Drained of tears, Jacob told Luke of their leaving Ohio and looking for a place to settle. He said, "Amanda's family had never accepted me as her husband. They said that I was not good enough for their daughter. When Suzanna was born they were even more angry with me."

"Families can be cruel," Luke said.

"We had both had enough and decided to head west and look for a new place to live and to make a home. We didn't realize how difficult this was going to be, and we made it this far before we got in serious trouble."

Luke nodded, not knowing what to say.

"What am I going to do, Luke? I can't make a plan. I don't want to leave her here alone. I don't want to live without her, but I have the girl to care for. I am at a loss as to what to do."

"Well, for now, Jacob, we will go to my home. We'll work out something. This child needs some good food and to sleep in a bed. Then she will know that she is all right."

All too well, Luke knew the agony of losing a wife, and he realized that Jacob would need time to face his loneliness.

In the morning, they broke camp, loaded the meager gear onto the horse and headed for the cabin.

Jacob had gotten up earlier to sit at his wife's grave and say his goodbyes.

Suzanna sat upon the horse as Lucas held her on the blanket rolls. She laughed as the branches slapped at her legs. She was too young to understand.

⌀

Sarah was surprised to see Luke back so soon. Quickly, he told her the story of the child and the woebegone man who returned with him. Tenderly, Sarah took the sleepy little girl from Lucas.

"Nathan, get some water from the creek and heat it. She'll sleep much better if she has a bath. I have some mush ready. Get me your other shirt to put on her. I don't want to look for her clothes tonight. Tomorrow I'll wash what she had on and see what else she has. I'll tend to you men as soon as I get her fed and tucked into bed. She's exhausted."

"Suzanna. What a pretty name for a pretty little girl," Sarah crooned as she bathed and dressed the little girl. Finally, after feeding her and wrapping her in Gramma's quilt, she turned her attention to the others.

"'Pears that Sarah has a mission," whispered Nathan to Lucas. "Maybe she won't be so set on cleaning now that she has Suzanna to take care of."

"Maybe she'll clean even more—there's more people to make a mess."

Sarah couldn't hear what Lucas and Nathan were whispering about, but she guessed. "I'll be getting more work out of you two."

Both boys grimaced.

CHAPTER TWENTY-FOUR

TROUBLE WITH
A CAPITAL "T"

"Luke, I've been here longer than you should have to put up with me. It ain't gettin' any better for me, and I'm just makin' all of you miserable with my mournful ways."

"I know you've had a hard time of it, Jacob, but you ain't wore out your welcome."

"I thank you, Luke, but even Suzanna has been more quiet than usual. I've got to get away and get myself straightened out," Jacob confessed as they worked the field.

"I've been studyin' on your dilemma, Jacob. If you don't mind my ideas about what you should do, I'll tell you what I came up with.

Jacob stood up and started to listen.

"I know how I had to go off and be myself until I came to grips with the fact my wife, Lizabeth, was gone. I had the children and had Gramma to watch over them. I went into the woods and dealt with my anger at losin' her. You ain't got no one to look after

Suzanna while you face your loss. Here's what I think. Leave the child here with us and get yourself straightened out.

"Oh, Luke, you've done enough already."

Luke continued. "No pain can last forever, and the sooner you deal with it the better. Nothin' will bring your wife back, and you ain't doin' your little girl any good frettin' like you are. We'll take good care of her and keep her safe until you come back."

"Luke, I just hate to burden you with another mouth to feed and a small child to take care of."

"It ain't no problem. Sarah will be happy to have the little one to care for. She's just a born caretaker. She's already been teachin' Suzanna to read her letters"

"I do see what you are saying about me getting away. I've been thinking that Amanda's family don't know what's happened to her. Even though they don't like me, they deserve to know that their daughter is dead. It's best I go back to Ohio and let them know that she died. That will give them something real to grieve over now.

"That does sound like a good idea."

"So it does. Maybe I can convince them that I'm not as bad as they thought. If you think it's all right, I'll leave my daughter in your good hands and go and make peace with Amanda's parents. I'll take the horse to make better time back. Then I'll return to get my little girl."

⚚

Ever since Jacob had left for Ohio, Lucas seemed to pay a great deal of attention to the little girl. "I found her," he said, "so I'm responsible for her. I must teach her to hunt and fish."

He took her to the creek and attempted to teach her to swim. The water was cold and she cried, "Please, Lucas, don't hold me under the water."

"But Suzanna, that is how you learn to hold your breath."

"No, Lucas, I'm afraid."

Since she would sit on the bank and hold a pole, she could learn to fish. But she wouldn't put the bait on the pole. And she found no joy in pulling a fish from the water. "The fish will die," she sobbed.

When he took her hunting and speared an animal, she screamed at the blood seeping from the animal's wounds. Then she would sob again, "No, Lucas, don't hurt the animals."

Lucas was beside himself with frustration. He was about to give up in disgust when he found a task at which she excelled. She could follow the bees to the honey tree. There was no fear in her as they smoked them out and scooped the honey into the birch bucket that Sarah had provided for them.

"I love honey, Lucas."

"Me too, Suzanna. Let's get some more."

One day, when everyone was busy at their jobs, she wandered off in search of more honey. She saw several bees heading into the forest. Disregarding caution, she followed them until she could no longer tell which way the cabin was. All she knew that there was a honey tree somewhere ahead of her. She had no way to light a fire with which to smoke them, so she decided to climb the tree to get at the cherished honey. Halfway up the tree she paused and looked down into the face of a small bear cub, also intent on getting the honey. She was terrified, and the five year old began to cry. "Please, Mr. Bear, I didn't mean to take it all. I would share with you. Please let me down from this tree."

It was a stand-off; the bear at the base of the tree, afraid of the sobbing child, and the child, clinging half-way up, thoroughly frightened by the bear. By this time, Lucas had missed her at the garden and had begun to search for her. He followed her meanderings into the woods and finally heard her loud sobs. He ran toward the tree shouting, "Suzanna! Suzanna! Where are you? Answer me so I can find you."

"Here, Lucas, here!"

Lucas saw the bear and figured out what had happened. The bear, frightened by all the racket Lucas was making and stinging from the impact of a well-thrown rock, loped off into the forest. Lucas hoped that the cub's mother was not nearby.

He reached up and took the child into his arms. "Suzanna, I have you now. You're safe. Let's go back home and tell Sarah that you found a new bee tree. You scared me half to death."

It seemed that Suzanna could not stay out of trouble. She was a naturally inquisitive child, and consequently she fell into the creek, rolled down the hill, stumbled on rocks, and almost scalded herself at the washtub where Sarah was boiling water for washing clothes. It was a full time job just to keep her out of difficulties. Most of the time, Lucas was her savior. He would threaten to tie her to the drying bush to keep her out of trouble. She would cry and say she was sorry, and he'd melt and hug her and let her go. Then she would get into something else.

One rainy day, Suzanna was missing. Sarah had looked in all of her usual play areas but could not find her. "Lucas, I can't find Suzanna. Please see where she might be. Honestly, that child is more trouble than all of the critters we have put together. At least I can tie them up when they get into trouble."

"Don't worry, Sarah, I'll find her." He set out for her favorite honey tree, but there was no sign of the little girl. Ranging farther afield, he began to call her name. He got to a rough area and saw a slip of rag caught on a bush. "She's been this way," he decided. He continued calling her name as he pushed his way through the heavy brush.

"Suzanna! Suzanna! This is not funny! You best let me know where you are hiding. When I get my hands on you, you are going to learn a lesson. I don't care what Pa says. You will learn to obey. I'm going to teach you. Now, stop fooling around and answer me.

"Lucas, Lucas," came a faint cry from somewhere.

"Where are you? I can't see you."

"Down here in a big hole."

Lucas caught himself as he almost stumbled into a sink hole. The cries were coming from it.

"Suzanna, are you down there?" he cried, trying to see into the depths.

"Yeth," she lisped. "I falled into the pit and I can't get out. It's all wet and muddy down here. Come and get me."

Realizing that he couldn't get to her without a rope, Lucas called to her. "Don't be afraid. I'll get you out. But first I have to get some help. Don't move. Stay right where you are. Don't try to get out by yourself."

"Pa! Nathan! Sarah! Help me get Suzanna out of the ground. She fell into a sink-hole and she says there's water in it. We must hurry before it floods and drowns her. As quickly as they could, they ran for the sink-hole, hoping that they would be in time. Sink-holes were numerous around the area. It was said that there was a big cave north of them, and this could be a part of it. The child could be lost to them forever if they didn't get her out immediately.

Lucas tied the end of the vine around his waist and began a cautious descent into the hole. "Suzanna, do as I say. Don't move until I grab your hand. Don't be wiggling around down there. Stay as quiet as a mouse."

With his heart in his throat, Lucas slowly climbed down, deeper and deeper. He couldn't see where he was going. He could only tell that he was getting closer to the girl because he could hear her breathing and sobbing. "Suzanna, I'm coming. Be still. Hold out your hand."

Groping around the slimy walls, he finally felt warm flesh. Swiftly, he pulled her close to him and tried to take a step forward. When he felt nothing but space in front of him, he realized how close she had come to disaster, and he clutched her even harder.

"Pa, can you pull me up? There's a big hole here and I can't see where I'm going. I've got her, but she's slippery from the mud."

"Lucas, do you want me to come and help you get her out?"

"No, it's too dangerous. Just keep the rope tight and I'll scale the wall. If we had another rope, I'd tie it to her and you could pull her out. Then you could pull me up."

"I've got another vine." Nathan called. "Let me throw it down to you. You can tie it around her and that will help. Be careful I don't hit you when it comes down."

"Wait, Nathan, I can't take a chance on losing my footing here to get the vine. I'll just have to do the best I can to get out without it. There's a deep chasm here, and I don't want to end up in it."

Finally, after what seemed hours of struggling to get up the side of the wall, moving forward a step or two and slipping back again, Lucas's head appeared at the edge of the pit. He used the last of his strength to push the child over the edge and into the waiting arms of Sarah.

"Suzanna, are you all right?" Sarah was so glad to see her safe that she didn't even notice how filthy she was.

Lucas just lay on the ground, trying to get his strength back. Suzanna understood that she had pushed as far as she could and that no longer would she be allowed to run wherever she wished. She had almost lost her life and almost cost her best friend Lucas his, as well. She went to him and put her arms around his neck.

"I'll be good, Lucas, I won't do anything bad again. I don't want you mad at me."

"I ain't mad at you. I'll just be glad when your father gets back and takes you with him."

"No, Lucas," Suzanna wailed. "I want to stay with you."

"Well, you can't. You have to go with your father."

Suzanna began to weep and, burrowing her face into his shoulder, sobbed forlornly, "I want my Mama."

It was the first time she had cried for her mother since she came to them.

CHAPTER TWENTY-FIVE

COCKLEBUR

Since Lucas had saved Suzanna from the sink hole, she had attached herself to him like a burr sticking to a goat's tail. No matter where he went nor what he did, she was always with him. It was getting to the point where he had no time for himself.

"Nathan, she's driving me crazy," lamented Lucas. "I can't even go huntin' that she ain't wanting to go with me. It's like she's another skin. I've got to get away from her."

Nathan thought it was funny to watch the little girl trying to keep up with the boy's stride as he went into the woods to get firewood or walked through the field dropping seeds into the furrows. Her short legs churned as she tried to keep up with the pace he set. For some reason, she decided that she was safe as long as she could see Lucas.

When Lucas went to hunt for small animals and finally got out of her sight, she would crouch at the edge of the woods and watch for his return. She became the bane of his existence.

"You gotta help me. I can't keep her in my pocket forever," Lucas moaned.

"The only thing I know is to find something for her to do. We'll have to find something." Nathan began to take pity on Lucas. "It was easier when she was getting into trouble every minute."

"Well, I don't want to crawl into a sink hole to save her, but she sure is more trouble now."

"Boys, I think Adam's comin' through the woods. Maybe he can help you," Pa observed.

After welcoming Adam and engaging in some small talk, Nathan said. "Adam, we got a problem with the little girl Suzanna." Then he related everything that happened.

Trying not to laugh, Adam studied what he had been told. "It seems as though she might benefit by having some animal to care for, one that was her very own responsibility. She could transfer her attention to it. Let me see what I can come up with. I'm heading for the settlement. Sarah, is there anything that you want me to bring from there?"

"Well, I could use some needles. I want to teach Suzanna how to sew."

"You might have to teach Lucas, as well," Nathan joked.

"I'll see what I can find. They are hard to come by, but maybe some needles came with the last trader. I'll be sure to get you some if they did."

"Thank you, Adam. I'm beginning to miss Sam'l's visits. You're the first person to stop by since the handfasting. Guess we won't be seeing much of Sam'l these days."

"I'll bet you miss his bringing you surprises, too," teased Nathan.

"Oh, Nathan, don't be silly. I don't miss his messing up the floor with his litter, either."

Adam thought about the surprises Sam'l had brought and what they had meant to Sarah. He resolved to do something about that.

Adam returned from the fort with a strange bulge inside his shirt. "What do you have that's moving around under your shirt, Adam?" Nathan questioned.

"Actually, it's something for the girls. I hope they like what I brought. I don't want to carry these again anywhere." He opened his shirt, and they heard a cheeping noise as the baby chicks he had carried tumbled out on the ground.

"Here, Sarah, these came from James. He had a time gettin' Martha to let go of 'em. She has enough left to take care of their needs, but she was trying to raise a flock. She talked a man going farther west out of a setting hen and some eggs.

"Oh, look at the babies," Sarah cooed. There were four little yellow balls of feathers peeping and scratching the ground. "We'll have to pen them up and watch so the foxes don't get them. Suzanna, go grind up some corn for them to eat, and give them some water."

Sarah could only think of the eggs they would get—and possibly roasting a rooster. Suzanna saw them as something of her own to play with and care for. Chickens grew fast. Soon they would be laying eggs and there would be more chicks to raise.

Lucas, as he watched the scene unfolding before him, breathed a deep sigh of relief, recognizing the chicks as the very thing that would keep Suzanna too busy to trail after him.

CHAPTER TWENTY-SIX

FAREWELL

A year had passed since Suzanna had come to them. Soon, her father would return to collect her. Sarah would miss the child, but she was resigned to the fact that she must rejoin her own father.

A few weeks earlier, they had received a letter from him telling them he would soon be there. Sarah had spent days preparing Suzanna to see her father. For her part, Suzanna could hardly remember him. She was now six years old and had to leave the only family she could clearly recall. She cried and said, "Sarah, I don't want to go. Who will take care of my chickies? They are going to miss me."

"Yes, they are. And I am going to tell them that you miss them, too. They will remember you. We don't know what your father has planned for the future. We'll just have to wait and see."

❧

A few weeks later, Jacob arrived. He looked well and was happy to see his little girl. He hugged her hard and saw that she had grown into a lovely child. Over and over again he thanked Sarah for her good care.

"I made my peace with Amanda's mother," he reported, "but her father still refuses to see me. In fact, he blames me for his daughter's death. I talked to several doctors back home who told me that there was nothing that could have been done to save Amanda. She would have died even if she had been in Ohio. It made me feel that I hadn't killed her by taking her into the wilderness."

"That should have made you feel better, Jacob," Luke said.

"A little. For a long while I blamed myself. Finally, I have made a decision to try to make up to Suzanna for losing her mother. I am thinking of staying at the settlement for a while. Later, I'll decide what I will do. I don't want to take the child away from you, but she belongs with me. If we stay close, it will make it easier for her."

Sarah nodded in agreement. Lucas was grinning.

"There's something else. Remember when the horse ran off with the herd? Seems she got with a male and has a foal. As soon as it's old enough to leave its mother, I want you to have it."

"Oh, Jacob, that's not necessary. You can keep the foal for Suzanna to ride," Luke protested.

"No, it's small enough payment for your taking care of my baby. I feel so obligated to you. There's no way I can fully pay you for what you did."

"That's not necessary, but we appreciate your feeling that way that you do." Luke would not humble Jacob by refusing his offer. He understood that sometimes it's harder to receive than give.

Sarah beamed. "Jacob, that is a mighty fine gift. I don't know if we're deserving, but we will accept your offer."

Both Nathan and Lucas grinned at Sarah's reaction.

Sarah was reassured that she would be able to see Suzanna from time to time—especially if she could learn to ride the new horse. It made the parting the next morning easier for her to bear as she waved goodbye to the little girl who had so stolen her heart.

CHAPTER TWENTY-SEVEN

TAKING STOCK

Sarah awakened and sat up on her bed. She looked across the cabin at the now empty bed of Suzanne. Tears welled up in her eyes. "I miss her already. She was a pest, especially to Lucas, but I really miss her."

For Sarah, life had not been easy, so in this moment of loss, she slipped into a reverie of taking stock of her life and all that had happened over the previous few years.

Truth be told, she thought, I am feeling sorry for myself this morning.

As a young child, Sarah had to leave her home in Pennsylvania and walk with her family to Kentucky County of Virginia to settle in the wilderness. Then tragedies seemed to pile up on her. It was a severe blow when her mother died. Sarah was very young and depended upon her Gramma to give her the support that she needed. Next, she was captured and held by the Indians, who had killed her Gramma and two younger children. In captivity, she was being groomed to become the wife of one of the braves. Eventually, though, she had been rescued by her father and Sam'l.

They had spent the entire winter in the fort with Martha and James in their small cabin. Finally, they returned to the site of their cabin, rebuilt it and accepted Lucas into the family. Sam'l remained a good friend, but he married Delia and they moved to his cabin, so she lost both of them. Next, she had developed a deep attachment to Suzanna, and now even the little girl was gone. Sarah continued to sit on her bed, feeling very sad.

She hadn't moved for many minutes when Luke came through the door, expecting breakfast. He was astonished to see Sarah still sitting on the bed in her nightdress. "Sarah, are you feeling sick?"

"Oh, Pa, I don't know. I just don't feel like doing anything." Sarah replied, her voice dull and flat.

"Well, it ain't like you to just sit. You'd have the fire goin' by now and the mush cookin'."

"I know, Pa. I was just sitting here feeling sorry for myself. Here I am, sixteen years old, and what have I got to show for it but hard work."

"Life on the frontier ain't easy, Sarah. You learned that long ago; it ain't changed none."

"I was a small child, Pa, when we came to the wilderness. That was your decision—and Ma's."

"I reckon that's a true statement. Your Ma and me decided that it would be best for the family to move out here. I thought we would all be happy and a family, but we really had some heavy hardships. Losin' Ma and Gramma was the hardest. I don't mean to say losin' the little ones was easy, but losin' your Ma was the worst thing I ever had to live with. I know that was hard on you, and I deeply appreciate how you took over from Gramma and helped us out. Why, we couldn't manage without you."

"I know, Pa. I would do whatever you need forever. But Nathan and Lucas are more trouble than they are worth, sometimes. It seems like they are intentionally messy and like for me to clean up after them."

"I know what you are sayin'," Luke replied. "I've told the boys to take care of their own cleanin'. It's a might easier with them living across the dogtrot. They ain't any cleaner, but at least they're not here except at mealtime to mess up this part."

"I just wish they would treat me different. They act like I'm their personal servant."

"I'll talk to them again."

"It's not just the boys bothering me that upsets me, Pa. I don't have any other women to talk to. I get so lonely out here in the wilderness."

"I don't know how to fix that, Sarah. When Delia was here and at Adam's you had someone close to talk to, but now she's moved farther away than the fort. Next closest place is the fort. You could see Martha or Traudel."

"I would like to see Martha. Traudel is all right except for her bratty son."

"And that is just the beginning of the problem; I don't want you to walk to the fort by yourself. For one of us to take you will use up three or four work days."

"How old do I have to be to go by myself to the fort?"

"Oh, Lord, Sarah, I don't know. You are just ripe for the Indians to take again. Just the thought sends shivers down my spine."

Lucas and Nathan burst through the door shouting, "What's for breakfast?"

Sarah and Luke were startled, as neither of them had made the fire ready nor got the mush cooking.

"Nathan, you poke up a fire and Lucas, get some wood. Let's give Sarah a hand this morning."

"The fire is usually started—what happened? Is Sarah sick? She looks all right to me. What happened?" Nathan asked.

"Just stir up the fire, Nathan."

Lucas needed no other orders; he went out the door and returned with an armload of wood for the fireplace. "Is something wrong, Pa?" he asked.

"Yes, Lucas, we need to talk about how you and Nathan can help around here."

"Help? We do everything we are supposed to do!" Nathan looked astonished.

"Sarah has been a mother to the both of you since you were little. She has taken good care of you without much cooperation from either of you. You are both messy, and she's expected to clean up after you. Her work is doubled by your carelessness."

"Pa, cleaning is woman's work." Nathan argued.

"Maybe so, but as of now, both of you are goin' to be more useful in takin' care of the inside of this cabin and of takin' care to put things where they belong. Soon, both of you will want to go off and stake your own claim and raise your own family. I don't know where you will find a wife who will care for you the way Sarah does." Luke's anger was starting to show.

Lucas stayed very still, watching, wide-eyed. He didn't know whether he should go out for more wood or just sit quietly and hope to go unnoticed. Pa's anger frightened him.

Nathan remained quiet, but he was bristling underneath. What had Sarah said to Pa that made Pa so angry? The men did all the hunting and fishing and most of the field work. All she had to do was keep the cabin clean and wash the clothes and make the things they wore and preserve the food for the winter and cook their meals and do the regular woman things. He was ready to leave, anyway, if he wasn't appreciated here. He could go and leave Lucas here. He could go live with Adam. Adam would appreciate having another man to help him with his work.

"Pa, I'm sorry, I didn't mean to cause a family row," Sarah apologized.

"Well, it needed to be said. We are all changin' and growin' up. Things will continue to change. The next few years will bring the greatest changes. I don't know what will happen. I just hope we can remain family and friends to each other."

"I hope so, too, Pa. I hope so, too," Sarah said.

CHAPTER TWENTY-EIGHT

RUNNING DEER

The next morning, Sarah, still feeling sorry for herself, wandered to the far side of the clearing to think. She sat down in the shade of a tree, and, while thinking, she chewed on a blade of grass. She had no idea how long she sat there lost in her own thoughts and nodding off every once in a while. A shadow fell across the ground in front of her. Startled, she looked up.

"Running Deer!" she gasped.

"Please, Sarah, no scream. No want to hurt you, please no scream." He held his empty hands in front of her.

Sarah was frozen into immobility. She just sat with her eyes wide open while panic spread throughout her entire body. She felt paralyzed.

"Please, Sarah, Running Deer no hurt you. Just want to talk. Please Sarah no scream, no run."

Sarah struggled to control her breathing. She managed a slight nod. She would listen because she was sitting down and really had no choice. She was bringing her fear under control and was deciding what to do next.

"Running Deer sorry for capture of Sarah. Please forgive. Running Deer like Sarah. Will not hurt. Will never hurt Sarah."

"What do you want, Running Deer?" Sarah finally managed to ask. "Where have you been? When did you learn to speak English so well?"

"Leave tribe. Running Deer still like Sarah. Running Deer still want Sarah for wife."

The shock of Running Deer's statement brought Sarah swiftly to her feet. Now panic was setting in again. What was she to do? She knew he was too strong for her to fight. He could outrun her. She was trapped. Running Deer, the Indian who had captured her when their home was raided, stood between Sarah and the cabin.

Running Deer seemed quite sincere. Sarah was trying to read his mind. Then Running Deer dropped to one knee in some kind of a gesture. Sarah saw her opening. She burst by him and ran screaming toward the cabin.

"Pa! Nathan! Help me! Running Deer is back!"

Nathan heard her. He stepped outside the cabin and saw Sarah racing toward him. The moment he heard the name, Running Deer, he ran into the cabin and grabbed his rifle. He sprinted out into the clearing, his eyes rapidly moving from side to side as he looked for a target. His sister needed his help.

"Where is he, Sarah?" Nathan shouted.

"Back there!" Sarah gestured toward the trees as she ran into the safety of the cabin.

Nathan went to the clearing and looked for signs of the invader. There was no Running Deer. Had Sarah dreamed she saw him again, or was he really out there in the forest?

BOOK FOUR

THE RIVER RUNS WIDE

CHAPTER ONE

HOMECOMING

Tap, tap, tap.

Lucas said, "What's that?" *Tap, tap, tap.*

"Again, what's tapping at the door?" Nathan asked.

"I don't know," Lucas said, "but I'll see."

"Knockin'! Nobody ever knocks out here," Sarah commented. "Lucas, go open the door and see if there is a woodpecker hitting on the cabin."

Lucas carefully put down the piece of maple he was carving and rose from his stool by the fire. "What if it's a big, black bear wantin' honey?" he teased.

Nathan laughed, "Either shut the door or give him your share."

Lucas opened the door just a crack, and his eyes bulged. "What in tarnation? What in tarnation are you doing here?"

"I comed back," a small voice said.

"What in . . .?" Nathan said.

"I comed back," the small voice said again.

Sarah rushed to the door. "Suzanna? My goodness, it's Suzanna! How did you get here? Where's your Pa?"

"Papa brought me. Oh, I miss you so much! Papa can't braid my hair like you did, Sarah, and I can't, either."

"You mean he brought you all the way from the fort just to get your hair combed?"

"No," laughed Jacob, appearing in the doorway. "I've come again to ask a favor of you and to tell you about the foal I promised. The mare you found when you saved us has had her colt. I wanted to tell you that as soon as she is weaned, I'll bring her to you. Suzanna decided it was time she saw her 'family' again. So I gave in and brought her along. We would have made it here earlier, but Suzanna had to stop and smell every wild flower we passed. She wanted to pick them and bring them to you, Sarah, but I convinced her they would only die before we got them here."

"Well, come in," greeted Luke.

"Can I get you something to eat?" questioned Sarah.

"I'm hungry," piped up Suzanna. "Sarah, I want some corn bread and honey."

"You are my Honey Girl," Sarah said as she prepared a hasty meal for the trail worn travelers. "I'll give you some after you eat your stew."

Luke sat back and watched the new arrivals. He sensed there was more to their coming than what appeared on the surface. When the time was right, he would find out.

CHAPTER TWO

DAUGHTERS

Jacob stood looking at his sleeping child curled up on Sarah's bed. She clutched the corner of Grandma's patchwork quilt in her tightly clenched fist.

"She's plumb tuckered out from gettin' here," Luke observed. "We have missed her. She always had to be in the middle of whatever was goin' on. I think her feet had a hard time keepin' up with her tongue. She is one chatterin' child." His work-worn hand gently smoothed her hair back from her face. "Reminds me of my little Mary. Mary would be almost as old as Suzanna if she had lived. Her grave's over there with the others. I thought that losin' Lizabeth, my wife, was bad, but losin' such a young child was almost more than I could stand. At least those renegade Indians didn't hurt her. They just killed her quick."

He tried to shake off the memories of his return to the cabin, happy with the game he had brought home to feed his family, only to discover the bodies of his two youngest children and Gramma in front of the burning cabin. The capture of Sarah and Nathan had slowly penetrated his grief, and getting them back gave him a reason for living.

145

Jacob sensed Luke's sadness and put his hand on his shoulder. "You lost so many more than I did, but you made a new life. Since Amanda died, I've been trying to make a life for Suzanna and me, as you did. That's why I'm here, Luke. I need guidance."

"I'll try to help, Jacob, but in the end, each man has to make his own decisions. What is it you are askin' me?"

"Let's go outside and I'll tell you."

They went outside and sat on logs close to the embers of the fire that Sarah had built to heat the water for washing clothes earlier that day. They gave off just enough warmth to take the chill off the air.

Jacob crossed his legs and began to speak. "Luke, it's been over a year since Amanda, my wife, died. You took care of Suzanna while I went back to Ohio to try to make peace with Amanda's family. You know her father blames me for her death, even though the doctors told me she would have died wherever she was. He never accepted me as being good enough for her. I realized that I couldn't live back there again, not with hate and knowing that her Pa would try to poison Suzanna against me, so I came back here to live. Suzanna had almost forgotten me. She was happy with you folks.

"We enjoyed takin' care of her, Jacob," Luke said softly.

Jacob hesitated, scratched his ear and said, "Suzanna is forgetting her Mama. She needs the care a woman can give her. I'm thinking of marrying again to give her a Mama, but all Suzanna can think about is that Sarah is her Mama. I know that Sarah is young, but she seems so much older than her years. I guess it's because she's mothered you and the boys for so long. So, I'm wondering if you would mind if I courted Sarah?"

"Jacob, that's a mighty powerful request." Luke was somewhat startled by Jacob's question.

"I know it is, Luke."

"Well, Jacob, are you askin' me if Sarah can be your wife and your child's mother? Like you said, she is very young, and it appears to me that you can find someone closer to your age than she is. She needs to have a chance to decide for herself who will be her life mate. Knowin' how much she loves your child could force her into makin' a decision that ain't right for her. I am goin' to ask you a question, and I expect you to answer me honest."

"I'd never lie to you, Luke. What is it?"

"Can you honestly say that you love my daughter for herself, or do you just want a mother for your child?"

Jacob found it very hard to look at Luke. He got up and paced back and forth.

"You don't have to say anything, Jacob. I can tell by your actions that you are not interested in Sarah as a wife but more as a mother for Suzanna."

"I reckon you are right, Luke. If I weren't looking for a mother for her, I don't rightly know that I'd be looking for a wife." Jacob admitted.

"I'll have to say no to your request, Jacob. It ain't fair to my girl. So while you are here, there can be no courtin'. So there won't be any embarrassment, we won't talk about this again."

"I respect what you say, and you're right about Sarah. Don't worry, I won't say or do anything to concern her. I'll leave in the morning with Suzanna if she isn't too tired from traveling here."

"There's no need to rush off as long as you don't say anything to Sarah about marryin'."

"Thank you, Luke. You are a good friend and a wise man. I'm proud to know you."

"I think once you get back to the fort, if you start looking for ladies there, you'll find a mama for Suzanna."

"I hope you are right. Good night, Luke. I believe I'll turn in and think about what you said."

"Maybe we could go to the Licks tomorrow. It will give Suzanna time to rest up before you head back. She's still a small child. You can get some salt to carry back to the fort. The ladies there can always use it, and you never know who you will meet."

𝄢

"Where's my Papa?" Suzanna asked when she awoke in the morning.

"He's gone hunting with Pa and to get some salt to take back to the fort with you."

"I'm not going to the fort. I'm going to stay with you," Suzanna stated firmly.

"You can go with your Papa and come and visit us sometimes."

"No, I can stay here and my Papa can come and visit us."

"But wouldn't you miss your Papa?" Sarah let her voice trail off, as she knew that arguing with Suzanna only made the child more resolute. She could tell from Susanna's set jaw that there was no moving the child away from her position.

Sarah, in order to divert Suzanne's attention, asked, "Would you like me to tell you a story?"

Suzanna responded immediately. "Oh yes! Tell me a story like you used to. I'll get the quilt. Remember how I picked out a patch and you'd tell me about it? You said it was a 'istry'"

"History," Sarah corrected. "One story, then I have to scrub the floor."

The little girl scurried to get the quilt. She studied it for several minutes before she selected one of the pieces. "This one." She chose a flower-sprigged section.

"That's a good choice. That piece came from the apron Gramma wore when she cooked."

148

"The Gramma who walked across the mountains when you came here and carried things on her back just like everyone else?" interrupted Suzanna.

"Yes, she was the best cook I ever knew. When I was still little and we still lived in Pennsylvania, before we came out here . . .."

"I never lived in Pennsylvania." Suzanne interrupted.

Sarah, used to Susanna's frequent exuberant outbursts, continued. "I remember the smells in her kitchen; it always smelled spicy."

"What kind of spice?"

"She and my Grandpa lived across the field from us on the farm. When Grandpa died, she decided to come with us."

"My Mama died."

Sarah pressed on with her story. "She used to make cookies for me. She made little gingerbread people. I was supposed to guess who they were. First, she would make one of Grandpa with a pipe in his mouth and a big smile on his face. I can't remember if Grandpa ever smoked that pipe. He always had it with him and he smelled of tobacco. When I smell tobacco, I always think of Grandpa."

"What does tobacco smell like?"

"Then she would make one of her wearing an apron and carrying a pie. Of course, I always guessed right, and she would let me lick the bowl when she finished. The next one was Pa holding a rake. She would put raisins on his face for eyes because she said he had sweetness in them when he looked at Mama."

"Did she make more cookies?"

"Yes, she made one of each member of our family. We never ate those cookies. We'd just hang them on the Christmas tree and sing carols about the family."

"What is a Christmas tree?"

"It is a cedar or fir tree that we would cut down and decorate for Christmas. Haven't you ever had a Christmas?"

"No, I don't think so," Suzanna said, pensively.

"Have you ever sung Christmas carols?"

"No, I don't think so. What are they?"

"They are songs about the birth of the Christ child."

Suzanna offered no response to Sarah's reference to the Christ child. She asked, "Can you teach me a carol?"

"Yes, I can, but that's for another day. Now I have to scrub the floor."

"Sarah," persisted the child, "do you wear her apron sometimes?"

"No, there is nothing left of it. It wore out, and Gramma cut out the good part and put it into the quilt. That's why it's a history quilt. Gramma said it was the story of her life. It's called a crazy quilt because it doesn't have a regular pattern, just pieces sewn together with fancy stitches."

"Can I make one? I want to have a history, like Gramma."
"Of course you can, and I have the first piece for it." Sarah went to the shelf and took down a piece of fabric. "This is from the dress I made for you when you first came to us. I made it from an old dress of mine, and I dyed it blue with the berry juice. I used the best parts to make you a dress. I'll keep half of it for my quilt and give you half for yours."

"Goody! Now, you have to teach me how to sew. I'll just have to stay here until I learn." Smugly, Suzanna made a statement of her intentions to stay.

Sarah knew better than to argue with her.

CHAPTER THREE

LOST

"Suzanna! Suzanna! It's time to leave," called Jacob. "Where is that child?"

"She was here just a bit ago. I saw her at breakfast, and that was just a while ago."

"She was going to help me clean up the dishes before she left," Sarah said.

"Then she can't be far away. Maybe she's saying goodbye to the animals. I'll go out back and look for her," offered Lucas.

After calling and searching for an hour, they still had not found Suzanna.

"She's hiding somewhere because she doesn't want to leave. Let's think about where she might have gone," said a worried Jacob. "She has to learn that she can't always have her own way. She'll have to be punished for this little escapade."

"We have to find her first," Luke commented, dryly.

"I looked for her in her usual places. She's not at the honey tree or with the chickens. I looked in the goat pen and behind Nibbles's lean-to. She ain't anywhere on the place," Lucas volunteered.

"She can't have gone far. Her short legs won't cover much ground." Nathan tried to be positive about her disappearance. "We'll just have to look for signs of a trail."

"That's going to be hard. She's been all over the place the last couple of days," said Sarah.

"Pa! Pa! It looks like she went into the woods over here. There's fresh signs," Lucas called.

"Sarah, you stay here in case she's just hidin' and comes back while we follow this trail. If she went this way, we'll bring her back," Luke instructed.

The men filed into the trees watchful for signs that the child had come this way. Each was concerned that she might have been taken by an Indian or attacked by a bobcat. Even though there had been no sign of either of them around, there could always be one renegade who had eluded their vigil. No one wanted to say that aloud.

Jacob, blinded by tears coursing down his cheeks, stumbled along behind Luke and prayed that Suzanna would be found soon. "If she wants to stay that bad, I'll find some way for her to be here," he silently vowed. "I can't lose her, too."

"Quiet!" Luke commanded. "Someone's comin'." He signaled the others to find concealment. Swiftly, they merged with the vegetation, leaving no sign that they had been there moments before.

Into a patch of sunlight that beamed through the ceiling of branches walked a man carrying a burden.

"Do you think you can walk a while? You are getting too heavy to ride on my back. We are almost there."

"Adam, it's you! And Suzanna!" shouted Nathan. "Where did you find her? How did you know we were lookin' for her?" Relief spread throughout the small band of seekers.

Forgetting his promise to punish her, all Jacob could do was to hold her and smother his tears of gratitude in her neck. "My baby! Thank the good Lord you're safe!"

"Papa, you're squeezing me so hard I can't breathe," protested Suzanna. "I ran away, and then I got mixed up. I was scared, I didn't know how to get back until Adam found me. I cried and cried."

"I was heading your way, Luke, when I heard her. So I just picked her up and brought her along. I came as fast as I could. I imagine that Sarah is about out of her mind with worry," Adam offered.

"Lucas," commanded Luke, "run on back to the cabin and tell Sarah the good news. We'll be along shortly."

"She's probably cleaned everything in and out of the cabin while she waited," chuckled Nathan. "When she worries, she scrubs."

"Well, it's too late today to head back to the fort. We'll have to wait until tomorrow," Jacob said. "Can we impose on your hospitality another night, Luke?"

Suzanna tightened her hold on her father's neck as he carried her back to the cabin. He would deal with her needs when he had to. Right now he wasn't about to let go of his precious burden.

After Suzanna had been safely tucked into bed for a nap, with Gramma's quilt again tightly clutched in her small hand, Luke and Jacob walked to the edge of the clearing. They sat on a log and talked.

"Luke, I just don't know what I'm going to do about Suzanna. She is so attached to your family that it breaks my heart to take her away, but she's my child and I love her."

"Jacob, you'll have to decide what's best for you. You know that we would care for her as our very own if you decided to leave her here. She would always be your child, but that is something that you will have to deal with."

"I understand what you are telling me, Luke. One decision I have made is to return to the fort and take her with me for the time being. Getting her there without a fuss may be a chore."

⌘

The next morning, a tearful Suzanna made her rounds with wet kisses and hugs for Sarah, Nathan and Lucas. She understood that she must leave the place she thought of as home and the people she had adopted as a family. It was as hard for Sarah to watch the little girl disappear into the forest with her father as it was for Suzanna to leave. The little girl kept turning around toward the cabin and woefully waving her hand in goodbyes.

"Oh, Pa, there are so many things I wanted to teach her. She's so tiny and so loving." Sarah could still feel the thin arms squeezing her neck in farewell and the quavering voice whispering, "I love you, Sarah."

"Her place is with her Papa. He's doin' the best he can by her. It ain't easy for him, either." Luke spoke from experience.

"I know what you're trying to tell me, Pa, but that don't make it easier to see her go."

"She'll be back." Lucas looked up from the stirring paddle he was whittling. "She may be a little girl, but she knows what she wants."

". . . and usually finds a way to get it," finished Luke.

⌘

On the way back to the fort, Jacob attempted a serious conversation with the child. "Suzanna, you are becoming a very spoiled little girl. I fear that it is my fault. I've been trying to make up for your losing your Mama, and I've been going about it in the wrong way. Now let's decide how we're going to correct that."

"Papa, I'm not spoiled. Look! No rotten spots on me." She held up her arms to show him her unblemished white skin.

"I didn't mean it the way you are taking it. You have a strong will, like your Mama's papa, and you need to learn to control that so you don't end up a bitter old person like he is."

"Do I know him? Where does he live? Why don't we ever go to see him? Do I have a Gramma like Sarah used to have?"

Jacob struggled to answer the questions. "They live a long way from here, back where we came from. Your Gramma hasn't seen you since you were a baby, and she would be very proud of the girl you have become."

"Then why don't we go to see her?" she asked with the simple logic of a child.

Jacob found himself unable to answer. He looked at the innocent eyes of the child for a few moments as he pondered what to say. After a while, he said, "Well, why don't we go to see her?"

CHAPTER FOUR

RETURN TO THE FORT

"Papa, don't forget my dolly Sarah made for me," Suzanna instructed Jacob as they prepared to go back to Ohio.

"I wouldn't leave your cornhusk friend behind, Suzanna. I know Sarah took special pains to make her for you."

"And I helped. I soaked the husks in warm water so she could work them, and I found a very special round nut to make her head. I even split vines to tie her arms and legs and make her hold together. I am going to show my Gramma how to make one. She can name hers Suzanna so when she looks at her she'll think of me when we are gone again."

"But maybe you'll want to stay close to your Gramma and Grandpa. You're the only family they have left."

"No, Papa, I'm the only family you have left. I'll stay with you and Sarah and Lucas and Nathan," She stated firmly.

"But we'll be far away from them."

"But just for a while. You promised Momma you'd make a new happy home for us. Then she died, but you still have me. Maybe Sarah can help us make a new happy home."

157

"No, Suzanna, we'll have to make it without Sarah. She can be your very special aunty. I'll think about your wants, and I promise to talk it over with you before we make a decision about where we'll live.

"We'll go home to Kentucky," stated the stubborn little girl. She set her jaws with determination.

⌘

Jacob and Suzanna stopped at Luke's to tell them of their decision to return to Ohio and to deliver the foal, as promised.

The new addition helped soothe Sarah's sorrow at knowing that Suzanna would soon leave.

"Her name is Jessie," Suzanna announced. "Keep her until I get back and get big enough to ride her."

"I'll be sure to take good care of her," promised Sarah. "Tell me all about what she likes to eat." Sarah tried to fill her mind with things other than the pending departure.

"She likes cookies, but I have to taste them first to be sure they are sweet enough for her. She likes them made with honey."

Sarah smiled at the attempt to wheedle yet another cookie from her.

"I'm going to see my Gramma and my Grandpa. Maybe my Gramma will make cookies like your Gramma did and then hang them from her Christmas tree so she can think of me when I come back here."

"Now, Suzanna, we don't know yet where we will end up. I guess it's going to depend on how your Grandpa acts when he sees you. You were a tiny baby the last time he saw you, and he is an angry man now."

"Why is he angry, Papa?"

"He wasn't happy about your Mama leaving with me over staying in Ohio with them. He didn't think about getting a son and

158

granddaughter, just about losing his only daughter to someone he didn't think worthy of her. Then, when she died, he got worse. He took out his sorrow in hating me. Now we'll see whether you will be able to heal his heart."

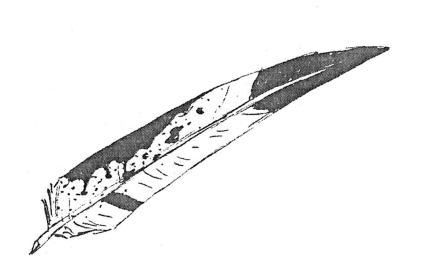

CHAPTER FIVE

A REVELATION

"Lucas, let's walk down to the creek."

"Sure, Nathan. Should we take our fishing poles?"

"We could. Maybe we will catch a couple of fish for Sarah."

The boys got their fishing poles and some bait and walked down to the creek. Lucas was waiting for Nathan to say something, as he knew that something was up.

Nathan was deep in thought. They finally got down to the water and baited their hooks, threw them into the water, and waited.

Nathan started. "Lucas, I've been thinking about going west. I'm getting more restless the longer I stay here."

Lucas broke into a big grin. "When do we leave, Nathan? I've been looking forward to this trip for a long time."

Nathan's shoulders slumped. "Lucas, I have to tell you something and it ain't going to be easy, but I feel that you are too young to go with me this time. I'm fourteen, almost fifteen, and you are only ten. I feel that you are too young to go.

"I'm almost eleven," Lucas said, sadly.

"I've thought about this a long time. I know Pa wouldn't let you go. He'd say you were too young. He'd be worried about you."

"I'm as good on the trail as you are, Nathan. Maybe better. Besides, Pa will worry about you, too. We talked a lot about the both of us going west."

"I know we did, Lucas. But this time I would like to strike out alone and go as far as the big river north of here. I'll be back for you and you can go with me next time. I really will, I promise."

Lucas knew he was out of arguments. He doubted that Nathan would come back for him. He doubted that Pa would let him go. He was in turmoil. He could run away and follow Nathan for a while before he let his presence be known. He wasn't sure how to deal with Nathan's change of attitude.

"How long do you reckon you will be gone, Nathan?"

"Can't rightly say. I reckon from here to the Ohio falls will take a month, and maybe I'll stay a month, and then the same for the return."

"What do you hope to see between here and the big river? More trees?"

Nathan laughed. "I reckon I'll see plenty of trees. This part of the world seems to be all forests. I want to make a chart of how I get to the river and how I can get back. Navigating through the forest is hard work."

"Well, you know I would be a help to you in tracking. I've got much more experience in tracking than you do."

"Lucas, I know that you would be a great help. I know you want to go. I know Pa would fret himself to death if you were. I know all these things, Lucas, but I still want to do this first trip alone. I'll be back, I promise."

Defeated, Lucas hung his head and watched the bobber on the end of his fishing line. He wasn't sure how he would deal with Nathan's departure. He knew in his heart that he would have to respect Pa's decision, as he did owe Pa his life, and he wouldn't go against his wishes under any circumstances.

Nathan was also quiet. He felt that he had betrayed his little brother. He didn't feel good about that. He knew he wasn't going to the river alone, but he would go with someone. He didn't know who. That would be decided later.

CHAPTER SIX

A HEART IS HEALED

"It's been a long, hard trip and you have been very brave, but we're here at last," declared Jacob as they neared the town. "First, we'll get cleaned up at the tavern and then go see about the reception we'll have at your grandparents."

"Can I wear the dress Martha made for me now?" questioned Suzanna. She had been eager to try it on and wanted to wear it to travel, but Jacob told her she had to wait until they got to her grandparents. He wanted her to present the best appearance she could to them.

"Of course, and we'll have baths at the tavern to get this trail dust and grime off of us. We'll just get all prettied up."

"Papa, you need to get your hair cut off and your beard, too. You look like a shaggy grizzly bear."

"You are right, child. You aren't the only one who needs to make a good impression. Martha put in a ribbon for your hair in the pack. We'll wash and comb you up like a china doll."

"What's a china doll?" queried the inquisitive little girl.

"It is the kind of doll your Mama played with when she was your age. Her Papa bought her everything he thought she might want. She was his very special little girl."

"Like I'm your special little girl. Does my Gramma still have the doll? Do you think she'll let me hold it?"

"I don't know, you'll have to ask her."

⚘

After securing a room in the tavern and having a bath in the hip tub, they were as clean as Jacob could get them. He had trouble trying to fix Suzanna's hair to her satisfaction. She told him that he couldn't braid it as smoothly as Sarah did and it looked straggly. The friendly barmaid achieved some success with Suzanna's braids. He finally took her by the hand, and they walked toward the house where she had been born. He breathed a silent prayer and hoped he was doing the right thing for Suzanna.

"There's the house—the one with the flowers around the front porch." They approached a neat saltbox cottage modified somewhat from the New England houses upon which it had been modeled. It had a softer appearance, with a front porch that seemed to invite a passerby to come and sit on it.

"It's a pretty house. It looks happy," commented Suzanna.

"Let's pray that it's a friendly house," said Jacob.

Letting loose of his hand, Suzanna ran ahead of him and fearlessly approached the front door with the confidence of all her six years.

"I can't reach the knocker, I'll just have to pound on the door," she observed.

She knocked, waited, and then knocked again. After what seemed a long time to her, the door slowly swung open. A man, leaning on a briar cane, stood there, looking out over her head. Slowly he lowered his gaze until he saw the child.

"Amanda!" he cried. An older woman came running to catch him as he staggered back in shock.

"It can't be. She's dead!" Tears coursed down his cheeks and he limped his way to a chest in the hall and sat on it, holding his grizzled, gray head in his hands. Sobs shook his bowed shoulders as he blindly groped for a kerchief to wipe his eyes.

Suzanna, seeing his distress, lost all fear and ran to put her arms around his heaving shoulders.

"You must be my Grandpa Trevor. I'm Suzanna and I came to see if you love me."

Slowly, the old man's vision cleared and he met her gaze with tear-reddened eyes. Even more slowly, his arms closed around her tiny body in a huge hug.

"You are her . . . made over. I thought you were my daughter come back to life!"

"I am your granddaughter. My papa brought me to make your heart heal."

"Where is he?" growled the old man.

"Here, sir." Jacob stepped forward.

Reluctantly, the gray veteran extended his gnarled hand to the trail worn man in buckskins. "Thank you," he finally managed to croak out over the lump in his throat. It was all that he could say before tears threatened again.

CHAPTER SEVEN

WELCOME HOME

Overcoming her shock at seeing these unexpected but very welcome guests, Suzanna's grandmother pulled her thoughts back to what was happening. It appeared that her husband was making welcome at their home the man he claimed to hate. She saw the years of hatred and anger at the fate that had befallen their only child fall away from the embittered old man. It was because of the candor of the child who stood in the circle of his once-strong arm. She saw how much the little girl resembled her mother and understood her husband's initially mistaking her for the child he once worshiped.

"I'm sure you saved a hug for your grandmother," she said smiling.

"Oh yes, I have been saving lots of hugs for you many, many years—all my life."

Suzanna ran to the round little woman who stood patiently waiting for her to be ready to come to her. With a shaking hand, she reached for a corner of the white apron that she wore over a plain, buff-colored linen dress. There was an edging of tatted lace around her collar, but other than that her clothing was unadorned. Her fine, white hair was pinned up in a bun and tucked under a filmy white cap. Tears of joy ran unheeded down her cheeks, which were pink like withered rose petals. Her soft lips silently mouthed words of thanks that the child she had so longed to see and hold was here and in her arms at last.

"Are you my Gramma?" Suzanna asked. "Do you bake cookies like Sarah's Gramma did?"

"I certainly am your Gramma. And I do bake cookies. Would you like one?"

"Yes, please, and I would like to taste cow's milk if you have any. Papa said cow's milk tastes different from goat's milk."

"Well, yes, we can take care of that right this minute. Come to the kitchen; you, too, Christian and Jacob. We have much catching up to do." She led the way to a cozy room with geraniums in pots on the window sills.

They sat around a trestle table that was brightly polished, sharing a pitcher of frothy cold milk and a plate of ginger cookies.

"You smell like Sarah said her Gramma smelled. Do you have a 'istry' quilt like she made? Can you make rabbit stew that tastes like 'brosia' like Sarah's Gramma did? Can you braid hair like Sarah does? "

"Slow down, Suzanna," Jacob whispered to his daughter.

She continued unabated. "Do you have time to make dolls for little girls? Can I hold my Mama's china doll?" Suzanna's tongue kept chattering with the questions she had waited so long to ask. She had thought about all the questions daily during the long trip to Ohio.

Granmma laughed. "Child, child, child, we will have plenty of time to answer your questions. Now you and your papa must stay here with us."

"Yes!" the grandfather said. "Yes, you must stay here."

Tears formed in Jacob's eyes. He felt as though a huge burden had fallen from his shoulders. He had wondered if his dead wife's parents would finally accept him. He knew that the way had been paved by the loquacious little girl who looked so much like her mother.

CHAPTER EIGHT

ABANDONED

"Papa, there's a wagon that's come in, and I saw some children," Suzanna announced as she found Jacob repairing the door on the storage shed at the back of her grandparents' house.

"Well, you may go and see if they need anything we can help them with. I'll be along in a few minutes, as soon as I finish this job. Maybe they are going our way and we might be able to hook up with them. It's time we start fending for ourselves. We've taken advantage of your grandparents' hospitality long enough."

"I already met the children. They have a wagon full of all kinds of things to sell. It's just the two boys and their mother. Come along and meet them," insisted the little girl, "they need some help."

"I don't suppose you'll let me alone until I do what you want. I'll finish this later." Jacob laid down his tools and followed his daughter to a cluster of people gathered around a wagon.

"This is my papa. I told you he would help you."

"What can I do for you, ma'am? My name is Jacob Ryhmer, and I'm visiting here from the Kentucky County."

An attractive young woman turned at his greeting. She was dusty and frustrated with the wagon that appeared to have a bent axle. One wheel was canted out at an odd angle. It was apparent that the wagon was not going any farther as it was.

"Hello, I'm Rachel Gilmoore and these are my boys, Thomas and Aaron. Boys, say hello to Mr. Rhymer. He's come to help us."

Jacob wondered what she was doing here without a man, but he was too courteous to ask. She obviously was a lady of quality, and the boys were mannerly. Thomas was about Suzanna's age and Aaron was perhaps two years younger. He wondered how she had gotten as far as Ohio alone.

She soon satisfied his curiosity, as he worked on getting the wheel off the wagon. "I'm sure you're wondering where my husband is and why he isn't here helping. It's quite a long story."

"After I get the wheel off, maybe we can sit on that bench and you can tell me as much as you care to—or what you think I should know."

It was close to dark before he finally got the wheel off. He had to unload the heavy wagon and prop up the bed of the vehicle before he could get the wheel loose enough to remove. Suzanna had run back to her Gramma's and had told her about the poor lady and her two little boys. Suzanna was told to bring the boys into the back yard to play while they waited for the axle to be fixed and to invite the lady to share dinner with them. Excited about her new playmates, she showed them the rope swing her Grandpa had hung from a tree branch for her. They were taking turns swinging when Jacob and Rachel arrived. Rachel had told Jacob that she would rather tell the story at dinner to all of them so she only had to tell it once.

At dinner, Rachel started to speak. "We, my husband and I, planned to take a wagon load of goods to sell in a store we wanted to start in one of the settlements. We were careful in what we chose to sell, and I must say we did a good job of picking quality merchandise. We joined a wagon train and started out. On the trail, my husband was rather careless and stepped into a badger hole and broke his leg. It was a bad break and the bone broke the skin. It became putrid and turned black, and he got a high fever. He was out of his mind with pain. I drove the wagon and tried to care for the boys while he raved from the pain. One night, he got loose and wandered away from the wagon train. The next morning some of the men and I found him. He just died. He was so sick that I don't know how he lasted as long as he did. We buried him and held a short service for him. It was too late for me to turn around and go back alone, so I just came along with the train. We got this far, then the axle bent." Rachel slumped over and started sobbing.

Gramma said, "Rachel, you have reasons to cry. That's more misery that you deserve."

"I'm sorry," Rachel said, "I guess I'm just feeling sorry for myself."

"No need to apologize." Jacob said.

"Girl," Gramma said, "you are worn to a nub. You will stay with us until you get some strength back."

"I truly appreciate you hospitality, I truly do," Rachel admitted.

Jacob was pondering the problem. "Maybe I can think of a way to help you, Rachel. Let me think about it some more."

"I'd be beholden to you, Jacob," Rachel said, quietly.

CHAPTER NINE

SAVED

A week had passed since Rachel and the children showed up at the Trevor's place. Jacob had straightened the axle on the wagon and was waiting for the blacksmith to finish a new rim for the broken wheel. While at mid-morning coffee, Jacob said to Gramma Trevor, "I think I have found a way to help Mrs. Gilmoore and me at the same time."

"Does that mean you will be leaving, Jacob?" Gramma asked.

"It does. We have to push on west where we started. I feel that we can hook up with Mrs. Gilmoore and help her drive her wagon to the fort. We'll just tie the horse on the back of the wagon and pack our gear on her back. Suzanna will have the boys to keep her mind off of the heat and bugs on the trip. Suzanna may even learn some ladylike manners from Mrs. Gilmoore, and best of all, she won't have to eat my cooking."

"Oh, Jacob! I know you need to have your own life, but I really don't want to lose Suzanna now that we've just found her."

"I know, Mrs. Trevor. I wish you could go with us."

Gramma sat upright. "Why, I'd never considered it. Who knows though? My dear husband, Christian, has improved so much since Suzanna has been here that he may decide that we should join you on that wagon."

"Oh, Gramma, would you truly?" Suzanna begged.

"Tush, child, we're too old for a trip like that," she protested.

"Sarah's Gramma was older than you are when she walked over the mountains carrying her pack with her 'istory quilt in it. Please come with us," begged the child.

"It's a history quilt," corrected Mrs. Trevor, "and it's too late for us."

"I'll talk to Grandpa and tell him I want him to come along."

Jacob and his mother-in-law exchanged glances. If anyone could get Christian Trevor to undertake a long hard journey, it would be Suzanna. She had a week to convince him.

ø

Christian had become a new man since Suzanna arrived. Suzanna became his shadow. He no longer used his cane to walk, and he had begun working in his garden again. Suzanna had learned the difference between a weed and a plant from him, and she had helped him plant a patch of greens for Gramma to use later. His attitude was improving, and he was no longer grumpy. Often they would sit on a bench at the edge of the garden, and he would tell Suzanna stories about her mother when she was a little girl.

One day, Suzanna remembered the china doll that her father had told her about. "Grandpa, do you remember the dolly my mama used to play with? I wonder if you still have it and if you would let me hold her?"

"Well, I believe it may be up in the attic. Let's go and take a look."

As they passed through the kitchen where Gramma was making an apple crisp for Suzanna's dessert, she asked, "Where are you two going now?"

"We're going to have an adventure in the attic," Grandpa said. "It's a trip to the past."

"Well, be careful that you don't start sneezing. It's dusty up there. Nobody has been in the attic stirring things up in a long time."

In the attic, Suzanna pulled a dress from an opened trunk and held it up. "My goodness, this dress would almost fit me."

"It was your mother's favorite dress. Let's take it down with us when we go. Maybe Gramma can make it over for you."

"Oh goody! Then I will have a new dress to show Sarah when I see her. What's in here?" Suzanna was busily rooting through old trunks and boxes.

"Oh, just things that I couldn't bear to part with or things that your Gramma thought she could use sometime."

"Grandpa, there's a book in here that has writing I can't read. It looks like a journal of some kind."

"That's the log I kept on the boat when I came to the colonies. I'd forgotten it was here. Let's take it downstairs with us."

"Oh, here's the dolly. She is beautiful!" Suzanna held up an elegant bisque doll dressed in brocades and satins of a forgotten era. "Did my Mama name her? Did she play with her and sing to her?"

"Yes, she named her Miss Matilda. And she was careful with her. Often she talked to her and called her 'sister'."

"Why didn't she talk to her real sister?"

"She didn't have one. She was our only child." Memories of his dead daughter brought tears to his eyes and sorrow to his heart.

He knew he would soon have to say goodbye to this child of hers that he had come to love.

"Let's go show Gramma what we have found." He closed the trunks and took her little hand in his. "Bring Matilda along; I'll carry the book and the dress."

"Look what we found, Gramma! Matilda looked so happy when I took her out of that dark, old trunk that she smiled at me."

"She would be very unhappy to have to go back into the trunk, since she has met you. Would you like to keep your Mama's doll?"

"You mean forever and ever? She is so beautiful, just like my Mama was. Oh, thank you, Gramma. I will take such good care of her."

"I know that you will, child; it is only right that you should have her. She belonged to your Mama, and now she is yours. Your Mama saved her for you."

"I wish she could talk and tell me about my Mama."

"Maybe she will, child. Maybe she will."

CHAPTER TEN

READY TO LEAVE

"**O**h, Papa, I wish Gramma and Grandpa were going with us," Suzanna said as they carried bundles to the wagon.

"Maybe we can come back to visit them again," answered Jacob, piling his gear onto the already laden wagon.

He stood back to be sure that it would hold the additional load. He checked the straps that held the barrel of water that would supply the needs of both people and animals when they left the river. Pots and kettles were hung on the sides, to be used when they stopped for meals. Most of the wagon was crammed with merchandize to be sold. A large canvas was attached to the side and would be unrolled and supported by poles at night for them to sleep under. There was no room inside the wagon for sleeping for any of them. The weather was still warm, so Rachel and the children would roll up in their blankets and sleep dry under the canvas. Jacob would sleep in the open unless it rained. If it did, he would take cover under the wagon.

"Here's one last package. It's some cookies for the children." Suzanna's grandmother caught up with them at the end of the street. "Jacob," she said, "thank you for coming to bring us such joy, seeing our Amanda's little girl. Please keep us in your lives. Now, Godspeed. Let us know when you have safely reached your home in Kentucky."

"We will, Mrs. Trevor. We will send a message back from the fort when we reach it. I've been wallowing in my grief, and now it is time to remember that I have a daughter who deserves a home and a father who is better than I have been."

"Yes, Jacob, it's time to let Amanda rest in peace and for you to make a new life for you and the child."

"I will," Jacob said as he started the wagon toward the West.

Gramma stood in the road, waving goodbye to the slowly lumbering wagon. She could no longer see because of the tears blinding her vision.

"It's time for us to let her go, as well," she sighed as she returned to the house, her husband, and her memories.

CHAPTER ELEVEN

ON THE TRAIL

"We have been traveling for many days now, I've lost track of how many. Shouldn't we be getting closer to the settlement?" questioned Rachel.

"Yes, I think we are getting close. Thank God, everything has gone smoothly so far. I guess the Indians have moved on to better hunting grounds. You know that Kentucky County was once their hunting grounds. As people moved in and began to clear the land for crops, the game became more and more scarce. You can't blame the Indians for resenting us."

"I suppose not, but they caused much heartache for the settlers."

"Yes, and the settlers caused much heartache for the Indians," Jacob answered.

"It's too bad that neither of them could negotiate a satisfactory settlement without warfare."

"True, Rachel, but that's what happens when two people want the same land. Well, they are not going to bother us now. Our worst fears will be the wild animals that are around here. Be sure to keep your boys aware of the dangers of straying away from the wagon when they are walking. I know Suzanna will wander after anything that catches her attention. I have to be especially watchful when she is walking. Wolves can be very daring."

Several nights later, howls woke them from their exhausted slumbers. Jacob quickly poked at the ashes of the dwindling campfire and threw some more fuel on it. "Rachel, keep inside the fire area. Don't wake the children; there's no need for them to be frightened. I am going to get more wood and keep the fire high. That's the only thing that will keep the wolves away. I'll bring the animals closer to the wagon and build a firewall around the animals and us."

"Where are you going? Please don't leave us alone. I am so frightened," Rachel sobbed.

"I need to get more wood. I won't be gone long." He picked up a long heavy stick and his shotgun in case he was attacked by a hungry wolf.

"Watch out behind you!" screamed Rachel as a lurking shadow sneaked up toward Jacob's back. Swiftly he turned and aimed at the beast, firing as he fell backward.

"I missed!" Jacob yelled. "He'll be back. I was off balance. I should have hit him with my stick. Maybe the noise of the shot will scare them off." Jacob hurried and got more wood.

Unfortunately, it did not frighten the wolves, and Rachel and Jacob were forced to maintain a vigil throughout the long night. Fortunately, the children did not waken, so they were not aware of the danger of the pack of wolves that was determined to feast on them.

As the sun slowly made its appearance, Rachel and Jacob were relieved of their sentry duty because with the coming of daylight the wolves gave up and slunk away. Both Jacob and Rachel, exhausted from the all night watchfulness, sank to the ground.

"Oh, Jacob, what would I have done without you?" Rachel sobbed.

"Rachel, we are in this together. It's good to have a companion."

"Let's wake the children and get started. If I had been alone on the trail, we would be dead by now. How can I ever thank you for coming with us?"

"We need to talk about this, Rachel, and this is as good a time as any while the children are asleep."

Uneasy, she looked with admiration at the man who had saved their lives and without whom she would be helpless. She owed him her attention and gratitude.

"Rachel, I don't know how you feel, but I have grown very fond of you. Last night showed me how much I miss a companion. It's been longer for me than for you, Rachel, to be without a spouse, but I hope you won't think I am forward."

"Oh, Jacob, I know what you are saying, but it hasn't been that long since my husband died. I don't know what to do."

"Yes, Rachel, your boys need a father, and my Suzanna needs a mother. You and I get along well. I know we could learn to love each other and we could be come a family. Maybe we could find a preacher on the way and get married before we get to the fort."

"Mama! Mama! You are going to be my Mama!" cried a delighted little voice. Suzanna had been awake and listening the entire time. "I'm going to have brothers."

"Oh, my!" Rachel blushed. "Well, since I meet your daughter's approval, I will have to consider your proposal," said Rachel, wryly.

"We can stop at Luke's before we get to the fort. We can be handfasted there. I want you to meet them. They are as much family as I have. I know Sarah will be a big help to you. Do say 'yes', Rachel."

"I am deeply flattered by you, Jacob. But let me think about it. It is a big step for me to take."

CHAPTER TWELVE

YES OR NO

The travel-weary group arrived at Luke's place just after noon. Jacob introduced Rachel to Luke. He could tell by the look on Luke's face that he was pleased that Jacob had come back with a woman.

Suzanna made a beeline to Sarah and chattered constantly. She was excited to be home with Sarah and tried to tell her about all the adventures of the past months in a few minutes.

"My grandpa Trevor made me a rope swing. Papa says when we get a claim he will make me one out here. Sarah, you can come and swing on it. I have my Mama's china doll. Her name is Miss Matilda and she is going to tell me stories of my Mama. I have to learn to write so I can tell my Gramma all about 'Tucky.' You can teach me tomorrow.

"We can talk about that tomorrow. Now, Suzanna, I want you to eat a bite and then take a nap."

"But I haven't told you all the news yet. Papa says he's going to make Rachel my new Mama, and he's going to ask your Papa if they can get married here like Delia and Sam'l did. They want to get married before they go to the fort so people won't talk, but Rachel isn't sure yet that she wants to."

"Suzanna, I do want you to settle down and take a nap," Sarah said, sternly.

Sarah's sternness was wasted on Suzanna. "Tell me a story to make me sleep. Tell me about Delia's wedding," demanded the child.

"If I promise you two stories tomorrow will you go to sleep now?"

"I'll try, but I'd rather have one now," yawned Suzanna.

"Just be quiet while I count to fifty, and if you're still awake I'll tell you a story."

"All right."

"One, two, three . . ."

By the time she had reached twenty-five, the youngster's soft, regular breathing told Sarah that Suzanna, the chatterbox, had finally given in to sleep.

✗

Rachel woke to the sounds of Sarah stirring the fire to prepare breakfast. Swiftly, she jumped from the bed.

"Oh, Sarah, let me help. I'm afraid I overslept. I was so comfortable. It's been a long time since I had the luxury of sleeping on a bed. It's full daylight."

"You were very tired last night. Suzanna and the little boys are still asleep. They are just worn out."

"Perhaps we can talk a bit. I feel I know you so well. Jacob has told me all about you and your family and what wonderful people you are. I think I can confide in you."

"Please feel free to say what you wish."

188

"I find myself confused. Maybe you will be kind enough to help me reach an answer for my dilemma," confessed Rachel.

"I will try, but I don't know how much help I will be."

They sat at the trestle table with mugs of tea, which Rachel had provided from the stores in the wagon.

"I have never tasted real tea before. I mostly use herbs to brew tea. This is delicious and such a treat. Thank you, Rachel."

"There are many things in the wagon that will be new or unfamiliar to the people out here. My late husband and I had hoped to start a trade store."

"A trade store." Sarah mused. She sat quietly, waiting for Rachel to sort out her thoughts.

"I guess I should start at the beginning. Eight years ago, I was married, reluctantly, to Evan Gilmoore, a well-to-do merchant with whom my father did business. He was many years older than I, but he was a good catch for a young girl without a dowry. My father wanted me to be settled before he died. He was very ill and knew that he had not long to live. He made an arrangement with Evan to care for me. In return, I was to be his wife. I was young and obedient to my father's wishes. I agreed, and my father died secure with the knowledge that I was taken care of, and, naturally, I went along with whatever my husband said. In his way, he was a good man but more of a father than a husband. When he died on the trail, I felt as though a burden had been removed from my shoulders. Now Jacob says we should be married to complete a family. Also, he is worried about people who will talk because we are traveling together. Sarah, I am attracted to Jacob, but I'm not sure that I want to be yoked to him as I was to Evan. I just don't know what to do."

"Oh, Rachel, I've never been married. I'm a poor one to judge your actions."

"I know, Sarah. I want to start a store in the fort and will need help to build it. I can hire someone to do the building. I have some money from Evan."

"Oh, Rachel, I don't know nothing about buildings or stores. Maybe Pa can help you with your answer. You can share your concerns with him. He has good judgment. You can talk with him later today."

ℰ

"Aaron feels really hot and says his head hurts," announced Thomas.

"Oh, my, I hope that he is not getting sick. We've imposed on you enough," worried Rachel.

"Let me see him. I have some herbs that might help him," Sarah said.

The little boy was scarlet and feverish. Sarah began to bathe him with cool spring water. She noticed that a slight rash was beginning to form on his stomach.

"I'm afraid that you will be here for a while. It appears that he may be coming down with measles. I'll use a poultice on him that will ease the itching, but this will just have to run its course.

Within two days, Thomas and Suzanne had also broken out with the disease. Both Sarah and Rachel were kept busy caring for the sick children. Jacob made himself useful by helping Luke on the farm and keeping buckets of cool water at hand for relieving the fever of the hot little patients.

Finally, all three children recovered and were fretful from their inactivity. Sarah was running out of stories, and Lucas had carved small, wooden animals for each of the children. They wanted to run outside.

"It's time for us to be on our way," decided Jacob. "We have imposed long enough."

Rachel heard the conversation and approached Jacob. "If you don't object, Jacob, can we wait just one more day?" asked Rachel.

"I suppose that you have a good reason for waiting," he responded.

"Yes." Rachel took Jacob by the hand and led him away from the others. "You have been everything that I could ask for in a husband during these past difficult days. The boys could not have a better father. You asked me to marry you, and if you are still of the same mind and wish to marry me, I thought that we could have the handfasting tomorrow before we leave," offered Rachel, shyly.

Jacob broke out in a big smile. "Oh, Rachel, you have made me the happiest man in Kentucky County of Virginia. I promise to be a very good husband to you and a good father to your sons," he vowed.

℘

The next day, with their children, Luke, Sarah, Nathan, and Lucas as witnesses, they jumped over the broom.

Suzanna was overwhelmed. She hugged Rachel and said, "You are my Mama now, aren't you?"

Rachel, with tears in her eyes, swept the little girl up and gave her a big hug. "Yes, and you are my little girl."

In a festive mood, Sarah prepared a small luncheon for everyone, then the new family started their trek to the fort.

As she watched Jacob, Rachel and the children disappear into the forest, Sarah thought out loud, "This was the second wedding in this cabin. Delia and Sam'l were married first, now Rachel and Jacob. I wonder. Who will be next?"

CHAPTER THIRTEEN

WEDDING GIFTS

Within a few weeks, Sam'l and Delia's cabin was beginning to look more homelike. Inside, there was a shelf near the door for the bowls and spoons. Pegs held clothing, and their sleeping skins now covered the vine-laced bed that occupied a corner. Sam'l pulled a drawing knife across the boards that were to become a table. Delia sewed, making winter moccasins for Sam'l. A cheery fire blazed in the fireplace, where a goose sizzled its fat into a pan beneath as it roasted on a spit over the flames. It looked and smelled like home.

There was a shout from outside. Sam'l opened the door to find Luke and Lucas, each pulling a travois loaded with bundles.

"Hello, Sam'l" Luke said. "We started out from home with one rack for Delia's trunk, her bench, and the packages Sarah readied for us. We stopped at the settlement and told them about you jumpin' the broom with Delia. They're all happy for you."

"We had another handfasting a week or so ago, too," Lucas said

"At your place? Really? Who was it?"

"It was Jacob and Rachel. They went to the fort to start a general store." Luke said.

"Well, that's wonderful. It's mighty good to see you and Lucas. Welcome to our home," Sam'l said as he eyed the amount of plunder that Luke and Lucas had brought.

"The folks at the fort recalled all the times they needed help and you were always willin' to lend a hand. So, what with all that Matthew, James and Martha pressed upon us, we had to build another travois to carry it all."

"I can't believe all that is for us. Delia, come and see what Luke brought."

Delia's eye widened, "Gracious," was all she could manage.

"We decided to bring all your things rather than wait for you to get them. It would have taken you more than one trip. Besides, Lucas has a special gift for Delia. I'm not sure what it is. Let's get unloaded before dark."

"It was thoughtful of you to come this far. I appreciate not havin' to go to the fort. Don't know what I'd have done about Delia. I couldn't take her, but I couldn't leave her," Sam'l said. They began carrying in the things that they had brought. Luke set the trunk on the floor just inside the door. "Where do you want this?" he asked.

"Just leave it there for now. I'll need another shelf built for my books when you get time," Delia said. "For now, I'll leave them in the trunk. It can serve as another place to sit until we get proper benches."

"Here's the packet of seeds from Sarah for your garden. She said for you to be sure you sow the gourd seeds; she labeled them all. I guess the only things she didn't tell you was which rows to plant with what seeds."

"This is special from her." Luke handed Delia a skin- wrapped package. She opened it to find a large hank of white woolen yarn.

"Oh, this must be from Nibbles, the sheep. When did she have time to spin yarn this fine? Last spring I helped her to card and spin the wool you sheared from him then, but it was nothing as soft and white as this," Delia marveled.

"She said she hoped you might have a special use for it soon," Luke said. Delia blushed.

"This is from Martha," said Lucas as Delia opened a package that contained dried apples, potatoes for planting, and a candle made of tallow. "Martha said Sam'l probably didn't bother with potatoes in his planting, and he might not have any put into the garden."

"How thoughtful of her," said Delia. "I guess she knew that Sam'l didn't worry about what he ate as long as it filled him. That's all changing quickly."

"James sent an axe head and a peck of corn. The bundles from Matthew contained a small bush. He called it gooseberry," Luke explained. "It has shiny, white round berries like big grapes, but they don't grow in clusters," he said. "They're kind of sweet. You can cook 'em or eat 'em off the bush. You know how Matthew is about growing things. You need to get it in the ground now and heap leaves over it, he told me."

"He said he'd have another bush for me to pick up on the way back," Luke added. "Sarah will be happy to have something sweet to cook for the boys."

"We used to have gooseberry pie back East. Tell Sarah that they take more sweetening than apples."

Lucas stood back from the three of them. In his hands was yet another bundle. He was uncertain about how to present it. Finally, he stepped forward, thrust it into Delia's hands, and said, "Here, I made it."

Carefully, she unwrapped the skin that covered a well-polished carving of a doe and her fawn. Every detail was clearly evident. They were lying on a bed of leaves, and she could see the veins in the leaves that surrounded them. It was a work of art, most lovingly made.

"It is so real, Lucas. It is the most beautiful thing I've ever had. Thank you."

Delia went to the shelf over the mantle, took down the bowls that were there, and gently set the wood carving in the place of honor.

The firelight reflected from the mellow tones of the wood, and the animals seemed to come to life. Delia thought of the talent that Lucas had. Surely there was a way to make that talent grow.

Lucas was satisfied that Delia was pleased. He would think about other things that would make her eyes light up as they had when she saw his gift.

CHAPTER FOURTEEN

TROUBLES

Sam'l and Delia had been in their new place since late August. Although they had made much progress, it had been too late to grow anything in the garden to store for winter provisions. Sam'l had hunted, and they had preserved as much of the meat as they could. It was a cruel winter. Many animals were starving to death. Even those people who had prepared for a long, cold winter suffered. To add to her discomfort, Delia found herself expecting a child. Sam'l was ecstatic about the baby. He couldn't do enough for her. Often, she wished he would do nothing. Finally, she said, "Sam'l, women have been having babies since Eve. I'm not the first, and, God willing, I won't be the last. Please let me live a normal life. I'm not going to break. I'm just doing what a lot of women do. I won't be sick every morning until the baby comes. It will soon pass."

She didn't know how wrong she could be.

Reacting to the unknown, Sam'l was beside himself with worry. He said to Delia, "I'm so ashamed of myself. I can't hunt and provide for you. I'm afraid to leave you, and I'm afraid to stay."

"Oh, Sam'l, we are in a bit of trouble. I wish we had closer neighbors. I hate to be so much trouble to you."

"Delia, you are not trouble. You are my wife. I can cook for you, but you must eat."

"I know, Sam'l; I just don't feel like eating."

"Even though the rabbits and squirrels are small and skinny, it is the best that I can do."

"I know, Sam'l. Even the deer you shot was thin and stringy. The only thing that was good was that I boiled it and made broth. That helped a little."

Sam'l decided that no matter what the cost he must get help for Delia. She needed nourishing food. He cut and carried enough wood to last a week and stacked it inside the cabin. When he was trying to ice fish, he saw a beaver swimming to its dam. It looked fairly healthy, and without hesitation Sam'l shot it, skinned it, cleaned it, and took it home.

Delia didn't ask questions about what kind of meat he had brought home. She just cooked it and they ate it. It did have a bit of fishy flavor, but neither of them cared.

Sam'l ate very little. He wanted to save the meat for Delia because he didn't know when he would next find meat. Delia used the last of the onions to flavor it. Sam'l hoped they would be able to save enough dried beans and corn for next year's planting. In the loft were those few potatoes Martha had given them for the garden. He would use those for food if he had to. He understood that he was responsible for two lives besides his own—Delia's and that of their unborn child. The responsibility lay heavy on him.

Just about the time Sam'l was becoming desperate, help arrived. Nathan, restless with being confined in the cabin, decided to put on his snowshoes and see what he could find for food. With little success, he hunted his way to the settlement. There he stopped at James and Martha's. He and James had some luck hunting. They found and killed a bear that was hibernating in a cave. It was not something they were proud of, but they needed food. James had insisted that Nathan keep the skin to protect him from the cold on the trail. Nathan would take none of the meat, as there were many to feed in Martha and James's cabin.

With her usual generosity, Martha had taken in three people who needed help. An older couple, Anna and Pieter Van Byrne, and their niece, Emma, were all of their family to survive. Emma's parents had died earlier in the year, and now Anna and Pieter were very ill and were afraid that they would never see home again. They were right; they succumbed to pneumonia within weeks of each other.

Emma now had no family and was alone in the wilderness. She was thirteen years old, a forlorn child. She had only Martha to love her and care for her.

℘

Knowing how short on supplies they were in the settlement, Nathan took only the bearskin and pushed on through the snow to Sam'l's. Sarah was concerned about her friend Delia. She had a feeling in her bones that all was not well with her. She had asked Nathan to check on her if he happened to be hunting near their place.

Half frozen, Nathan arrived at Sam'l's cabin. He had wrapped the bearskin around himself, so when he pushed open the door, he looked like some frost-covered monster.

He threw back the fur and was recognized. When he saw Delia's big eyes staring from her thin face, he knew it had been right to come. Her swollen belly told him that she would deliver a child. She looked sick. Sarah's feeling had been right. He had to find a way to help.

199

Nathan looked at Sam'l and saw a look of desperation that Nathan had never seen on Sam'l. "Sam'l, my friend, what is wrong."

"Oh, Nathan," Sam'l said, sadly, "I fear that we are mighty nigh to starving to death. I can't leave Delia to hunt. I don't know what to do. I am mighty glad to see you."

Nathan warmed himself by the fire. "Sam'l, one of us can hunt while the other stays with Delia."

"I'm greatly relieved to see you, Nathan, and I'll go hunting first thing in the morning."

"I'm thinking, Sam'l, that first we need to get help for Delia. There's a young orphan girl at the fort who is living with Martha. She is a young Dutch girl, but Martha has her hands full trying to keep her own brood going. Emma could come out here and help Delia. She could stay with Delia while you hunted."

"I'm afraid to leave Delia to hunt. She's been so sick. I truly would like the help if Emma's willing, but don't know how we can feed another person."

Nathan could see Sam'l distress. He said, "Sam'l, why don't I go back to the fort and see if Emma would come out here."

"I would truly appreciate that, Nathan, truly I would."

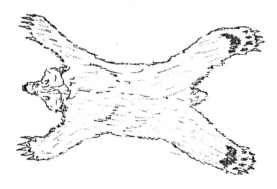

CHAPTER FIFTEEN

SNOW IN THE AIR

Surprised, Martha said, "Nathan! Are you back already?"

"I am, Martha. Things are not good at Sam'l's cabin." Nathan told Martha all the details of Sam'l and Delia's life. He painted a grim picture and put urgency in his voice.

Martha was greatly moved and prepared some herbs that, when brewed into tea, would ease Delia's nausea. Then they discussed the idea of taking Emma to help Delia with the chores and to be with her while Sam'l hunted.

The three of them sat down and talked about Emma's going to Sam'l's cabin. Emma was happy to be needed and wanted to go where she could do some good. Martha was kind and had never made Emma feel that she was a burden, but she knew how hard it was for Martha and James to keep their own family fed.

Nathan explained, "The snow is deep, and it is cold. Emma, the trip will be long and dangerous. I will walk fast and you will have to keep up. Can you do that?"

"I will surely try, Nathan."

All the villagers knew that Emma would need warm clothing for the trip and to live at Sam'l's. They put together an outfit that would keep her from freezing on the way. One article was the scarf that had belonged to her aunt Anna. It was long and could be wrapped several times around her head and neck.

Nathan packed wool into the bottoms of her moccasins to keep her feet from freezing. He wrapped her hands with rabbit skins. The only thing they didn't have was food. He would have to solve that problem as they traveled.

Finally, they were as prepared to leave as they could be. Nathan strapped borrowed snowshoes on her feet and instructed her in their use. Until she got used to them, walking would be difficult.

Nathan was anxious to get Emma to Delia as quickly as possible. Taking a young girl on the trail was not something he looked forward to. This trip would be hard, even for an experienced woodsman. He hoped that she could hold up. He gave last minute instructions. "Emma, it looks like snow. Try your best to keep up, 'cause we want to make as much distance as we can. Dark comes early this time of year. I'll look back at you every now and again to see that you are still with me."

Emma nodded. During the first hour on the trail, Emma stumbled and fell several times as she tried to master the snowshoes. Finally, by following immediately after Nathan and imitating his gliding movement, she made better progress.

Nathan tried hard not to be impatient with her slowness and clumsiness. It was not good to be unsheltered overnight in the cold. He had known that travel would be slower with her, and he planned to reach a cave that he knew of before nightfall. At this rate, they would get there later than he had planned.

As they traveled, he was constantly watching for a sign of game. At last, in desperation, he killed a hawk that was also looking for food.

A grove of pine trees offered some shelter from the cold. The small fire over which they huddled while the bird cooked seemed only to emphasize how cold it was. The sky was darkening, and Nathan's senses told him there would be an unexpected and unwanted snowfall. He had to decide whether to stay where they were or to try to reach the cave. If they stayed where they were, they would surely freeze. If they pushed on, they might reach safety. There was no doubt in Nathan's mind as to his course of action.

"We have to go, Emma. We can eat while we walk. I'm afraid we are in for some snow, and it's going to be a good one."

Emma's muscles had tightened up as they rested. It was painful for her to pick up the pace that Nathan set. She clenched her jaw and forced herself to move as quickly as possible. Before they could drop on the ground, tears of pain froze on her cheeks.

Softly, silently, snowflakes began to fall. Soon, they were walking through a wall of feathers. Visibility became so difficult that it was hard for Emma to see Nathan if he got too far ahead. She was afraid of losing him.

"Nathan! Nathan! Wait for me," she cried.

He stopped and waited for her to catch up. "We must hurry before the snow gets so thick I can't see the trail. We need a vine or something to hold us together."

"I've got my scarf. We can use that. You take one end and I'll hold on to the other."

They struggled through the growing drifts. Emma followed blindly. She held onto the scarf for dear life. She stopped abruptly as she ran into Nathan.

"I think the cave is around here close. Everything looks so different when it's covered with snow," he said. "I just hope there isn't a bear in it."

Eventually, he found the opening. Gratefully, they stumbled into the dry darkness. "Should be some tinder close to the opening. Feel around the floor for some shavings. Don't let go of the scarf, though."

"Here's some," she called.

"Good, now we can get a fire goin'. There's logs cut. I've stopped here when I've hunted. Everyone who uses a cave leaves a start for a fire for the next person. It sure comes in handy times like these," Nathan answered. "At least we won't freeze, though we ain't got nothing to eat."

"I just want to be warm. Missing one meal ain't goin' to starve us," Emma answered.

In a few minutes, Nathan had small flames started. He carefully blew upon them and fed them until the small fire could be increased with logs. The fire gave light as well as warmth. Emma could see that they were in a small cave. The ceiling was low. Nathan could stand upright only in the very center. Because the cave was so small, the fire took the bitter chill from the air. It was still cold, but they would not freeze unless the fire went out.

Emma dropped to the floor in the cave. She was exhausted. She curled her body into as tight a ball as she could and lay as close to the fire as she could get. She was so cold that she thought she never would get warm. She began to shake uncontrollably. Her teeth chattered together from the cold.

"I'm so cold. I can't feel my hands or my feet," she cried.

"Here, let me rub your hands. Maybe that will help. Put your feet 'round to the fire."

Slowly, feeling came back into her hands and feet. She was still cold, but she had stopped shaking.

Nathan put another log on the fire and stacked logs behind Emma. She slept fitfully. Their lives depended upon his keeping the fire going.

The snow stopped falling before dawn. The mouth of the cave was partially closed up with it. It helped keep the heat inside.

Nathan scooped some snow onto a piece of bark and let it melt. Emma awoke and drank the melted snow he offered her. He had been outside the cave and scouted the area.

"We can get through the drifts. They ain't as bad as I thought. It'll be slow, but we need to get going."

CHAPTER SIXTEEN

SPRING AT LAST

Nathan and Emma finally reached Sam'l's cabin, bringing a rabbit that had been too weak to escape his sling. Sam'l and Delia were overjoyed to see the pair, as they had worried about them being out in the blizzard. At one time, Sam'l had said that he thought he should go out and try to find them. But then, he was in the same dilemma—who would take care of Delia?

Now that Nathan and Emma were back, Sam'l was more free to try to find food. Delia would not be alone, and with the medicine that Martha had sent, Delia was no longer as ill as she had been. Nathan hunted farther afield than Sam'l did. Sam'l wouldn't go more than an hour's distance from the cabin.

❦

Finally, the severity of the weather lessened. Delia was becoming clumsy as her body became larger. Emma was helpful, eager to do whatever she could to please Delia. She worried that after the baby came Delia would not need her around, and she didn't know what would happen to her then.

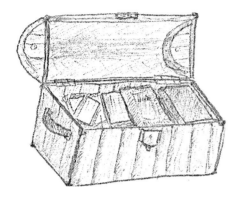

To fill the long winter days, Delia taught Emma from her books. Emma loved learning, and she quickly absorbed all of the knowledge that Delia presented. She questioned Sam'l about the local animals and birds and soon learned to identify them by their tracks and sounds. Nathan taught her about the roots and berries that were safe to eat. She listened much and talked little.

After the snow melted and the soft young shoots began peeking from the thawing ground, small animals ventured out and soon grew fat by eating the new growth.

Nathan and Sam'l were able to keep meat on the table, and Delia and Emma prepared to plant a garden.

"Before I leave, Sam'l, we should try to get a deer for you. I know how you don't like to go far from Delia now. We can make some jerky, and with that and what you get fishing and hunting close by, you should get through the birthin' time. Those fish we caught smoked good. Emma knows what greens to pick and where to find roots to dig. That'll help until the garden is ready. I need to get home to help Pa with the spring plantin'. I'm going through the settlement on the way home. When should I tell Martha to come?"

"Delia reckons it should be about six weeks before she will need her. I got enough to do around here, so Delia won't notice I'm hovering. I just can't help worrying. I ain't never been a father before. Matter of fact, I ain't never been around a real baby. I'd rather face a mad grizzly bear than be here without knowing what to do. I am so happy that Emma is here to help when Delia gives birth. I feel so helpless," Sam'l confessed.

Nathan felt the same way but didn't admit it. He was getting uneasy about being there when Delia's time came. He remembered being sent to the creek to fish when Ma had the last baby. Pa told him to keep Sarah and the other two children there until he came for them. Gramma had been able to help Ma. It seemed like such a long time ago. Having babies was woman's work, and Nathan wasn't about to be around when they did it.

Having prepared as well as they could, Nathan was free to go, and, after the goodbyes were said, he hastened to leave.

Trotting toward the settlement, Nathan, moving at a distance-eating woodsman's lope, quickly covered the miles. On the way back, he stopped at the cave and replaced the wood that he and Emma had used. No telling who might be in the same situation that they had known. He stopped at the settlement long enough to return the borrowed snowshoes, remind Martha of the impending birth, and to be assured that she would go to Delia in six weeks. Thus assured, he headed for his home place. He planned to help Pa plant the corn, then he would head for Adam's place and help him clear another field. It would give him a good excuse to stay with Adam. He had enough worry about women to last him a long time. Sarah would question him about Delia until he didn't have any answers left. Life would be much simpler without women, he sighed. He was anxious to get to Adam's cabin, where there were no women.

CHAPTER SEVENTEEN

THE WAITING

During the winter days, when he could not get out to hunt, Adam had worked on his cabin. He built a cabinet in the corner to hold the skins that he had cured and stacked. When the weather broke, he would keep what he needed and give the rest to Delia and Sarah.

He had everything he needed to be comfortable. He wrote in the journal that he had kept for years. Often he sat and played his flute. He didn't know he was lonely until Nathan arrived.

"Nathan! It's really good to see you again," Adam said, enthusiastically.

"It's good to see you, as well, Adam. I helped Pa plant the corn, and now I have some free time. I reckon you could use some help."

"I truly appreciate that. First, I would like to clear another field, then I would like to plow and plant a garden."

Nathan was more than happy to help Adam. He wondered why Adam planted a garden, but it wasn't up to him to ask.

Adam had built a roofed porch on the front of the cabin and set a rough bench on either side of it. Skins were stretched to dry on racks that leaned against the sides of the cabin. Hanging from the eaves of the porch was a net made of vines. Adam used it to scoop up the fish that he caught from the stream.

It was a comfortable, homey place. Delia had transplanted a wild rose from the field, and it had climbed up the rock chimney of the fireplace. When he went to Sam'l's, Adam planned to take a cutting from that rose for Delia to plant at her new home. Adam still missed Delia.

Nathan had told Adam of Delia's condition, and together they worked on a surprise for her. When they figured she was safely through her ordeal, Adam would take the gift to her. He would put the gift on a travois and haul it to Delia. But he would wait some time before going, as he didn't want to be there for the birthing process.

ɓ

Adam and Nathan hunted and fished together. They were becoming fast friends. Nathan often spent the night at Adam's cabin, and Adam more often visited Luke's cabin. Each time he visited, Adam realized that he missed Delia more than he could have believed. He confided in Sarah, who was very understanding. Finally, he and Nathan made an agreement. Nathan would stay at Adam's cabin and tend the fields and garden for him while Adam went to see how his sister was. By this time, he should have a new nephew or niece.

Sarah had added her gifts to those that Adam was taking to Delia. She sent gourds that she had bored holes in for Delia to use as birdhouses. The purple martins would nest in them and eat the mosquitoes that were so plentiful. Also, she had woven fabric for Delia to sew into baby things, and she knitted a soft shawl in which to wrap the baby. She had made a tiny pair of moccasins, as well. Nathan said they were so small they wouldn't fit his fingers.

Pulling the loaded travois behind him, Adam left for Sam'l's cabin. He was prepared to stay a week or so and help Sam'l. He was not prepared for what he would find when he arrived.

CHAPTER EIGHTEEN

SURPRISE

Sam'l was stretching a skin on a rack when Adam arrived. A girl, whom Adam assumed was Emma, was hanging clothes to dry over the bushes. From the number of white squares that he saw, Adam knew that he was an uncle. From the cabin came the sound of humming. There was a stack of freshly cut poplar trees near the cabin.

"Welcome, Adam," called Sam'l. "Delia is inside with a surprise for you," he beamed. Adam propped the travois against the cabin and stood inside the door, allowing his eyes to adjust to the sudden change of light. Delia sat on a bench next to the fireplace. She held a bundle in her arms, her foot steadily rocking a cradle.

Adam was puzzled. Why would she rock the cradle when she held the baby in her arms? Had its birth addled her thoughts? Sometimes that happened, he knew.

Sam'l came to the door behind Adam. Delia looked up and smiled, "Adam, it is so good to see you. It has been such a long time."

"It is good to see you too, Delia. I'm anxious to meet my new niece or nephew."

"Meet your nephew, Adam. His name is Eli."

Adam grinned at the new baby.

"Now, meet your new niece, whose name is Kate. Eli and Kate, this is your Uncle Adam."

Adam was flabbergasted. "Two of them? There's two of them? What are you going to do with two of them?"

"Why, keep them, of course," Delia laughed.

Adam sat down on a chest. He felt he had better sit before he fell over in a faint.

"Here, Adam, take Kate while I feed Eli."

"I never held such a tiny baby. I'll drop it."

"Her, not it," Delia corrected.

"Just put your hands out. It's easy once you make up your mind not to be afraid," Sam'l said.

"I'm not afraid. I just don't want to hurt her." Again Adam backed off.

Sam'l expertly took the tiny girl from Delia and cradled her in his arms and said, "Adam, did Martha not tell you we had twins? They were a week old by the time she got here. I helped Delia. It was the most holy experience I've ever had. Delia was wonderful. She never screamed and . . ."

"Please spare me the details of the birthing," Adam protested, "I don't intend ever to find out, so I don't need to know about it."

Adam couldn't believe that this rough woodsman, Sam'l, could be reduced to such a bundle of worship by these two bits of humanity. Why, even in blankets they looked like picked chickens. He looked closer at the baby Sam'l held. The blanket covered part of her face. Adam put out a hesitant finger to move the blanket so he could see her face. A tiny flailing fist hit his finger and four tiny fingers and a miniature thumb instantly closed on his finger and captured his heart.

Gently, he tried to disengage her grasp. She held on tightly. Somehow, without his realizing how it happened, he found himself holding the infant. She opened her unfocused eyes and made a sucking motion with rose petal lips. Adam watched her, bewitched.

CHAPTER NINETEEN

A BEAUTIFUL MORNING

Nathan had made his breakfast and walked outside of Adam's house. "So this is what it is like to own your own cabin and be the master of your own castle," he thought. No, Nathan didn't own the house, it belonged to Adam who was visiting Delia, but it felt like his as he languished in the luxury of silence. He looked at the woodpile and decided it would be good exercise to split some wood for the fireplace.

Nathan took the broad axe and was splitting some logs when he heard a strange voice behind him.

"Hello at the cabin," the voice said.

Nathan turned around to see two young men about his age standing at the edge of the property. Both men were carrying long rifles; both wore coonskin caps.

"We come peaceful," the one boy announced

"We mean no harm," the other responded.

Nathan, with his mouth agape, stood with his axe in his hands and looked at the boys. He knew he couldn't run to the cabin and get his rifle. If they were going to shoot him, they could do it.

"Can we come forward?" the taller of the two asked.

"We mean no harm," the other reassured again.

"Yes, yes, come on up," Nathan finally said.

Both boys came forward and the taller extended his hand to Nathan and said, "We are the Matthews brothers. I am Robert, and this is my brother David."

"I am pleased to know you," Nathan said. "We don't get much company out here, and I was took aback when you spoke to me. I am Nathan Reed."

"Mighty pleased to know you," David said as he shook hands with Nathan.

"We don't have many people that are just traveling through," Nathan remarked, his voice filled with curiosity. "Where do you hail from? I mean where did you come from?

Robert, who seemed to be the older of the two, spoke slowly and carefully. "Our parents immigrated to North Carolina when we were just children. In fact, David was so young that he doesn't remember the trip from England. Last summer we got the wanderlust and started out for the West. We made it through the gap by late fall and then we got jobs as hired hands on a farm; that carried us through the winter. Earlier this spring we lit out and have been traveling north and west ever since. We don't rightly know where we are now."

"Well," Nathan paused and thought. "I don't rightly know where we are either. I know this is Kentucky County of Virginia. I know where the fort is and Sam'l's place. But I don't know much else." Nathan hurriedly corrected himself. "What I do know is these woods. I've hunted them ever since we got here from Pennsylvania."

"Pennsylvania? That's a far piece from here," David mused.

"Yep, it is," Nathan acknowledged.

"Do you know the way to the Ohio River Falls?" Robert asked.

"No, I've never heard of them. Maybe Sam'l would know them."

"Who is Sam'l?" Robert asked.

"Sam'l is a woodsman and tracker. He has been all over these parts. He talks about the big river. I am going to the big river sometime soon. But I don't know when. I have a little brother who wants to go along, but I've convinced him that I need to go alone this first trip. He is too young yet . . . but traveling a long distance alone is a little fretful."

Robert nodded his head. "Yes, it is. I'm glad I have David to travel with."

"I'm glad I have got you, too, big brother."

"I've forgot my manners. Did you eat today? Do you need anything?" Nathan asked.

"Well," Robert drawled, "We ate yesterday, but we are low on provisions. We don't mean to impose on you, but we could use some food."

"I'll fix you something. Then, as you eat, you can tell me why you want to go to the Ohio River Falls."

"Shucks, that's easy. The ship owners pay money to have their goods portaged down the falls. We heard that boats can't go down the falls loaded with cargo. So all goods have to be carried for a half mile or so," David explained.

"What we heard is that the boats come down river to the falls. Then the passengers and cargo are taken off. Then the boats skim over the Falls and dock downstream. The cargo has to be carried down to the dock downstream. Workers are paid cash money," Robert explained further.

Nathan was hooked. "Cash money? How much?"

"Don't rightly know. But, we're going to give it a go."

"This your place, Nathan? Do you live alone?" David asked.

"No, this place belongs to a friend, Adam. I live with Pa, Lucas and Sarah about a half day's walk thataway," said Nathan, gesturing to the northeast.

"Where's Adam?" Robert asked.

Nathan laughed. "Well, Adam is at his sister Delia's. Delia is Sam'l's wife. They just had a child and Adam went over to see it. The fort is between here and Sam'l's. We have lots of friends at the fort."

Embarrassed, Robert explained, "We don't mean to be nosey. It is just that this land is new to us, and we are lost and passing through. I hope you won't mind the imposition. We really mean no harm."

Nathan served some cornmeal mush. "I do understand. I am curious too about what's out and beyond this area. I am anxious to see the big river. You can stay here a few days before you travel onward."

"We are much obliged," David said. "We are a bit tired of travel and if it won't put you out too much, we could use the rest."

And so the three of them settled into a long morning and afternoon of talking as they continued to cut and to stack wood. The wood pile grew tall. Nathan trusted the boys. They seemed friendly and honest. Long into the night they talked, then they rolled up into their sleeping skins and slept soundly.

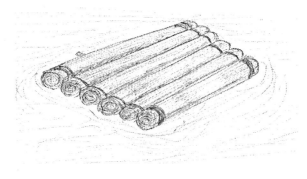

CHAPTER TWENTY

A NEW IDEA

At dawn, all three boys staggered outside and built a campfire. Robert seemed pensive. "Nathan, I've been thinking. You could come to the Falls with us. You have been wanting to go to the big river. That is, after Adam gets back."

Nathan's mind was sent spinning. "Oh Lord, how I would like that! But, I'd have to talk to my pa first. I couldn't leave without telling him that I was going and getting his blessing."

"We can go to see them with you," David offered.

"What would that all entail?" asked Robert.

"Well, first of all, we would have to walk about a half day to my pa's cabin. That is our home. Then I would have to talk with him and see how he feels about me going off to the big river. Then I would have to tell Lucas. That won't be easy. I don't think Sarah will care one way or the other."

"It's early morning here. We could tidy up this place and be on our way. We could be at your pa's by sundown," David ventured.

"That's true, we could be. There isn't much to do here. Just clean up and shut the door. Let's do it!"

⚮

Walking at a quick pace, the boys ate up the miles in no time. They talked about the upcoming trip. Nathan was very curious.

"Robert, how did you learn so much about the rivers and geography?"

"Robert graduated from the grammar school," David said, proudly.

"I did," Robert said. "I was a good student and I had a good teacher. I learned as much as I could because I knew I was going west someday."

"Tell me about the big river again. I don't really understand it. Nor do I know how the states are situated. I know that I was born in Pennsylvania and we came to Kentucky County when I was young. My ma died, and I ain't been partial to books."

"What you call The Big River, I believe is the Ohio River. I know it starts in Pennsylvania and goes along Ohio. I know it is a long river, almost a thousand miles long. I also know that it empties into another bigger river, the Mississippi. I don't know how long that river is, but it ends at New Orleans and probably goes up the middle of the country, maybe as far as the North Pole. What I do know is that, if we want, we can take a boat from somewhere on the Ohio all the way to New Orleans. What an adventure that would be!"

Nathan was dumbfounded at the new information. His mind wandered, and he became engrossed in his own thinking and exploring.

Robert continued. "Nathan, the state where you were born goes east toward the Atlantic ocean. If you go south from Pennsylvania across Virginia you get to North Carolina. That is where we are from."

Nathan was trying to understand Robert's description of the states when David whispered, "Stop," they all stopped as David raised his rifle, aimed and fired.

"What did you shoot, David," Robert asked.

"A deer," David answered.

"I didn't see it," Nathan admitted. "You are good in the woods."

The boys reached the deer and spent the next hour field dressing the animal. Then they cut it in half so it would be easier to carry. They didn't have far to walk. Within an hour they came to Nathan's home.

℘

Sarah had just poked her head out of the cabin door. She saw the boys and queried, "Nathan?"

"Hello, Sarah, We shot a deer on the way. Meet Robert and David Mathews.

Sarah didn't respond. She was busy looking at Robert. She saw that he was tall, with dark hair, blue eyes, and a beautiful smile. He was very masculine.

Robert bowed to Sarah, "Pleased to meet you, ma'am."

David also bowed. Both Nathan and David could see that Robert and Sarah were in a world of their own. Neither was aware of anyone else in their surroundings. Nathan had to ask twice, "Sarah, where is Pa?"

"Oh, oh, he's in the corn field with Lucas." Then she stepped back inside to catch her breath and fan her red face. "Oh, my!" She said to herself.

℘

The boys had just finished dressing out the deer when Pa and Lucas came up. "What have you got there, Nathan?"

"We shot a deer, Pa. Meet Robert and David Mathews."

225

"Proud to make your acquaintance. Where do you boys hail from?"

"We're from North Carolina," they both said in unison.

"Mighty long ways from here, ain't it?" asked Luke, having no idea where North Carolina was. "Where you boys off to?" Luke continued.

"We're heading for the Ohio River and the Ohio River Falls," Robert explained.

Luke had no idea what Robert was talking about. He was in a dilemma. Should he show his ignorance? Yes, he thought. "Where is the Ohio river?" he asked.

"It's north of here. I believe Nathan called it the big river."

"Oh, yes, I've heard of it. In fact, when we rescued Nathan and Sarah from the Indians, we were close to the big river."

Both David and Robert looked startled. "The Indians?"

"Yes, we'll tell you of their capture and escape after we eat our evening meal. Sarah will have to put some extra vegetables into the stew. We always have enough."

Lucas had been standing by, listening to everything. He knew that he had not heard the last of the big river story. But what was the mystery?

CHAPTER TWENTY-ONE

THE QUESTION

"Pa, can we talk for a minute?" Nathan asked.

"Sure, son, let's take a walk."

"Pa, the Matthews boys are going to the Ohio River to a place called the Ohio River Falls. That's a place where boats can't go down the rapids fully loaded. So, they have to unload and have someone carry the cargo down the slope to another dock, where it is put back on the boats. They pay cash money for a day's work."

"That's good for the Matthews brothers, but I feel there is another question following."

"Yes, Pa. I would like to go with them."

"I figured as much."

"Lucas can help you while I'm away."

"You're not taking Lucas? I wonder how he is going to feel about that?"

"We talked about it once before. He's not happy about my decision, but I think he is too young to go with us."

"I quite agree. Son, if that is what you want to do, I won't stand in your way. When will you be comin' back?"

"I will be back by corn picking time. That's a promise."

❦

Sarah and Robert were sitting on a log not far from the campfire. It was far enough that no one else was privy to their conversation. It was obvious that they were enthralled with each other. Sarah had not met many younger men her age.

Back around the campfire, Luke spoke up. "Robert, if you are interested in the story of Nathan and Sarah, this is a good time to tell it."

Robert and Sarah got up slowly and joined the group. Luke related the story of Sarah and Nathan's capture and how they were rescued. He told how they had captured Running Deer, but somehow he had escaped from the fort. He had been seen upon two occasions near the cabin. Sarah was still afraid of Running Deer, who had been captured by the Indians when he was a young child and who thought of himself as an Indian. Then Luke told how Lucas had joined the family.

Robert asked, "You mean that Running Deer is white but thinks of himself as an Indian?"

"Yes, we believe that is what happened." Luke continued telling the story.

Both Robert and David listened attentively. Robert and Sarah would exchange glances and shudder at the close calls that the family had endured.

Finally, Pa said, "It's about bedtime. Nathan, Lucas, Robert and David can sleep in the other cabin, I'll sleep in the other bed in the main cabin. "Now, you boys be careful about traipsin' around at night. I sleep with my rifle at my side and I don't want to shoot anyone accidentally."

Robert and David took Luke seriously. Nathan and Lucas knew Pa didn't sleep with a rifle at his side, but they saw his point.

☙

The next morning dawned bright and clear. All four boys were up and stirring at the campfire, trying to get it going but not having much luck. The coals were wet from the light rain that had fallen overnight. Actually, there was no need for a campfire. Sarah was making breakfast at the fireplace in the cabin. Nathan and Lucas knew better than to enter the cabin without Sarah's invitation. David and Robert hung back politely.

The door of the cabin opened. Sarah poked her head out and said, "I've got corn meal mush that you can sweeten with honey, and I've got potatoes in the coals."

The boys started for the cabin, Nathan first. He wiped his shoes on the skin by the door. Then Lucas did the same. Both David and Robert parroted the actions of the other boys. They both realized that staying on Sarah's good side was a must.

"Good morning, Sarah." Robert said.

"And good morning to you, Robert," Sarah sang, "and to you, too, David."

The boys filled up on cornmeal mush topped with honey. There was little conversation, as all three boys were thinking about leaving. David was anxious to leave. Nathan was apprehensive and busied himself thinking of everything he needed to take to sustain himself for a few months. Robert was having second thoughts, as he was quite taken with Sarah. Sarah was equally enamored with Robert. Luke was a silent observer.

"Do you know your plans for traveling, Nathan?" Luke asked.

"I reckon we will go back to Adam's place and see that everything is all right. Then we will go to the fort and get some supplies that we—or Robert and David—don't have. I reckon then we will go to Sam'l's place. We need Sam'l to tell us how to get to the big river, the Ohio River, from his place."

"After you get to Sam'l's place, do you know how much time you will need to get to the Falls?"

"I rightly don't, Pa. Do you know, Robert?"

"I reckon a week should do it," Robert answered. "But I'm not sure."

"I wish I could go with you as far as Sam'l and Delia's place. I would really like to see the new baby. I have some other gifts for her," Sarah said, hopefully.

Luke spoke up immediately, "I'm sorry, Sarah, but that is out of the question."

Sarah just looked down. She didn't argue. She knew that Pa wouldn't change his mind.

⌀

It was just after noon when the three boys started for Adam's cabin. Their walk through the woods was uneventful. Robert shot a rabbit for their evening meal. Everything was as they had left it in the cabin, and Adam had not returned. The boys made themselves comfortable, roasted and ate the rabbit.

"Tomorrow we will go to the fort and on to Sam'l's. It will be a long day, so we should get some sleep and try to get up before daybreak. We want to be on the trail at first light."

"Good idea, Nathan," David said.

Robert seemed to be lost in his own thoughts. Neither Nathan nor David bothered him. They just got their sleeping skins ready and went to sleep. Robert eventually did the same. A girl with a long, golden braid wandered through his dreams.

CHAPTER TWENTY-TWO

PLANS IN THE MAKING

"Adam, this swinging cradle you and Nathan made is wonderful. Right now, both Eli and Kate can fit into it, but it won't be long before they have to take turns. What a good idea this is. I can hang it from a tree limb and not worry about their being where I can't see them or hear them when I'm working outside." Delia was thrilled with the gift.

"We'll make another one for Eli," Adam said.

"Eli's older than Kate, so don't you think you should make another for Kate?" Delia teased.

"I know I'd better help Sam'l build that room on before I worry about cradles. You sure need another room in the worst way. It's a good thing the weather's warm so I can sleep outside. There isn't room in the cabin. I'd have to sleep standing up."

"You are right about that. Since the babies' cradle takes up the space where Emma slept, she's been sleeping with me, and Sam'l's slept on the porch. We've got all the food drying in the loft, so Emma can't sleep up there. When we put the room on, Sam'l and I will sleep there and leave Emma and the babies in here by the fire.

Later on, we can put up another chimney, but for the time being we'll just pile more skins on the bed to keep warm next winter," Delia explained.

"Maybe you won't have to do that. If you gather up some stones, maybe before snowfall, after the crops are in, Luke and the boys can come with me and we'll put up a chimney. Then you can all stay warm," Adam said.

"Oh, please bring Sarah along. We'll have the other room, and it won't be too cold for you men to sleep in. Oh, I'd love for her to see my babies. I want her to meet Emma, too. She is closer to Emma in age than I am. Maybe she can get Emma to talk to her. Emma is so very quiet and unsure of herself. She needs to build confidence. She is so smart and so pretty, and she tries so hard."

"I'm not sure they can all leave their place at the same time, but we'll work out something," Adam promised. He went to stack cornerstones for the new room.

⍦

"Hello, Sam'l," came a shout from the edge of the clearing.

Adam and Sam'l were wrestling a heavy plate log in place. They both looked up, surprised. "It's Nathan!" Sam'l said. "I thought he was supposed to be at your place."

"I guess he isn't. He has two boys with him."

As Nathan approached he said, "Sam'l, Adam, meet my friends Robert and David Matthews."

Robert, who was carrying a deer, extended his hand to Sam'l. "I am proud to know you, and you, Adam."

"Well, what in tarnation is going on? What are you boys up to?" Sam'l asked, bewildered.

"It's a long story, Sam'l, but we'd like to stay here a day or two. We'd like to make some jerky out of the deer and we'll leave the rest for you. Adam, your place is fine. Lucas or Pa promised to see about it every few days. We can help build your room. But the short story is that we are heading for the Ohio River. We want to work at the Ohio River Falls—for cash money," Nathan explained, breathlessly.

"Whoa! You three are going to the Ohio River Falls? Does Luke know?" Adam asked.

"We went home to ask Pa. Then we got my traveling gear and went back to check on your place. It was all right. Then we went to the fort and onward to here," Nathan explained.

Sam'l shrugged his shoulders. "Well, I reckon, if it is all right with your pa. We can use the help in building the new room. We got all the logs cut, so we can set the joists for the floor and tomorrow we can begin raising the walls."

Adam said, "With the additional help, I believe that we can start putting a chimney base in now, too. It would save a lot of work later on. Let's get the base stones from the river."

Delia appeared at the doorway. "Nathan, I have something I want to show you."

Nathan approached the cabin door, knowing he would see an infant. He was totally shocked when he learned there were two babies. "Oh, Lord, won't Sarah be surprised. Robert, David, come here and see these babies."

Delia then introduced Emma to the boys. Emma was very shy and stayed out of the way as much as possible. She would steal a glance at Nathan every once in a while. Nathan, of course, was unaware of this.

ॐ

With five men working, they made quick work on the new room. The top logs were the hardest to put up, but Sam'l had rigged a sort of pulley that made lifting them much easier. While Sam'l, Robert and Nathan worked on the roof, David and Adam worked on the fireplace. They got the chimney base built on the outside of the cabin. The rest of the chimney would have to wait until later. Delia and Emma began chinking the spaces between the logs and packing them with wet clay. This room, too, would have a loft. Delia planned to have it filled with supplies in case the winter was as bad as last winter had been. She wasn't about to have her babies go hungry.

Within three days, the new room was nearly completed. Sam'l could floor it when he had time. Meanwhile, tamped dirt would serve as a floor. The boys had made a supply of deer jerky. They were ready to leave in a day or two.

Adam took his rifle down from the side of the new room. He was ready to leave and return to his own claim. Somehow, the way the sun struck the new clay chinked into the logs caught his attention. He looked more closely at it and an idea began to form in his mind. When he got back to his cabin, he planned to consult the journal he had been keeping long before he came to the wilderness. It contained entries of information that he had thought might be of value to him out there.

Meanwhile, Nathan, Robert and David were getting information from Sam'l on how to get from his place to the Ohio River Falls. Sam'l gave clear directions and also much advice on how to deal with people on the river. He said he had been to that area once, but he thought that it would be much more developed by now.

In the morning, Adam would go one direction to his own home, while Nathan, Robert and David would go in the other direction, north to the river. Sam'l, Delia, Emma and the twins would remain at home. Sam'l's heart would be going along with the boys.

CHAPTER TWENTY-THREE

A NEW PROJECT

"Luke, did you ever know anybody who made bricks?" Adam asked.

"No. I do know that they are made from clay and have to be fired in a special oven. I've seen one of those. They look like a beehive. Why do you ask?"

"I noticed the clay we used to chink the logs at Sam'l's. The way it was drying made me think it could be used for bricks. There's a man I met up around West Point who knows about making them. I think I'll go to see him and get some information. The corn won't be ready for picking for another month. I've pulled my garden beans, and I can do without the rest. It'll take a couple of weeks to get there and back. If you could just keep an eye on things at my place, I'd appreciate it."

"We'll do our best. Either Lucas or I will check every once in a while"

✒

A few weeks later, Adam and a stranger returned to Luke's place. Behind them straggled four spindly goats.

"It took us longer than I'd planned," greeted Adam. "These animals can be very stubborn. We had six when we left West Point. We dropped off two at Delia's. Here's two for you, and I'll keep the other two. Luke, this is Ike Brandon. He knows all about bricks, says there's a certain kind of clay that is the best to use. He is going to look around at what we have. There's a layer of it over at Sam'l's. I think we have some here, too. I'm interested in making some bricks."

"Why?" asked Luke.

"Well you haven't been to the settlement in a while. People are moving out here so fast, it's hard to believe. Why, there's a claim being settled 'bout every five miles from here to there. It's getting crowded, and people are wanting more than log cabins to live in. We've got our share of clay, so I figured we might as well make bricks out of it. Clay won't grow anything. It might as well be useful for something."

"What do you think of our clay, Ike?" Luke asked.

"You sure got enough of it," Ike commented. "I'll know more once I look around."

"Oh, Pa," called Sarah, "Come quick! There's animals in my garden eating everything in sight. Hurry! Where did they come from?"

"They came from Adam," Luke said. He started grabbing the lead lines that trailed from the neck of each goat. The voracious animals had eaten through the branch Adam had tied them to and were enjoying the tempting garden.

"Goats are good eating, and you can drink their milk or make cheese from it," Adam explained.

Sarah didn't know whether to be happy with her gifts or to cry because they had destroyed part of her garden. She admitted that it was thoughtful of Adam to bring such a welcome source of food. Sometimes he reminded her of Sam'l. She did wonder how she would be able to keep the critters out of her garden. They smelled bad, too. How, she wondered, could she wash a goat?

Lucas wondered what the cheese tasted like. He would make sure nothing happened to the goats until he found out if the cheese was as good as honey.

CHAPTER TWENTY-FOUR

CHIMNEY BUILDING

One by one, the travelers came though the woods. Each carried a pack. Luke and Adam had a second hanging cradle between them. Luke led the way and Sarah followed him; Lucas brought up the rear. "We came to finish your chimney."

"You look like a parade," Delia laughed.

"Where are the babies?" Sarah had only one thing on her mind. She was anxious to see Kate and Eli.

"How could all of you get away at the same time?" Sam'l questioned.

"Ike Branden's staying at our place," Luke answered. "He's building an oven to make bricks. It's called a kiln. He found some good clay 'bout halfway between our place and the settlement, so he's starting a claim there. Goin' to start makin' bricks as soon as he gets set up. He ain't even goin' to cut logs for a cabin. He's goin' to use his own bricks to build the side walls."

"It was Adam's idea to get him down here. If it works out they'll start a brick-making place. Guess Adam don't got enough work on his claim to keep him busy," Sarah said.

"Wish we had some bricks here. These rocks get a might heavy when you have to lift them very high," Sam'l said. "We got the base built the last time you were here, Adam. There's a pile I brought up from the creek to finish the chimney. I've been waiting to cut the hole in the wall for the fireplace. I didn't want to leave it open for critters to wander in and out of our cabin. With all your help, it ain't goin' to take long to fill the hole with the chimney."

"Pa, can't it wait a while?" Sarah begged. She wanted to be with the babies as long as possible.

"Sarah, take some time to see the babies, but remember, it ain't right to take advantage of Ike's help. We'll need to get back as soon as we can. It ain't right to expect people to take on our responsibilities longer than we have to," Luke answered. "Have a look now, then you can play with Kate and Eli in the evenings."

"Come in, Sarah. Meet the new babies," Delia said

Sarah went into the cabin and met the twins. Delia also said, "Sarah, this is Emma. She has been with us since shortly before the babies were born. She is a Godsend."

Emma blushed and said, "Hello, Sarah. Delia has told me about you. I am pleased to make your acquaintance."

"Likewise, Emma," Sarah said.

"Oh, Delia," Sarah continued, "your babies are so very precious."

✍

Later, with Lucas mixing clay and straw to put between the rocks and Luke, Sam'l and Adam setting the stones, the chimney rose rapidly. They used larger stones closer to the ground, and as they moved upward they used smaller stones. Even Sarah was pressed into handing up the smaller ones.

"I'm wondering," Adam said, "if we should stop about half way up and finish the rest with brick. It would be good advertising for Ike."

"It would be a lot easier than trying to get these stones to fit," Sam'l said. "But," he continued, "it would be another month or so before we could finish the chimney. I don't want to wait that long."

Luke had built a makeshift platform half way up the chimney for Sarah to stand on. Lucas would hand her the rocks from the pile on the ground and she would hand them to Luke on the roof. Adam mixed the clay in a bucket, which Sam'l pulled up with a vine rope. They were working well as a team. When one bucket was empty, Adam would go and get water from the stream and prepare another clay mixture.

The work had stopped as they considered building the rest of the chimney with bricks. Forgetting that the flat log on which she stood was unsteady, Sarah became unbalanced, slipped, and fell to the ground. As she fell, she tried to catch herself. She hit her arm on a log. It made a sickening thud. Sarah knew her arm was broken even before it began to hurt.

"Pa, what am I going to do?" She sobbed with frustration after Luke had splinted the break with a trimmed branch. "I've got all the winter supplies to lay in, and I can't use my right arm. I can't even hold the babies."

"I don't rightly know, Sarah," Luke said, sadly. "I wish Nathan would come back soon; we really need him now."

"I could go fetch him, Pa" Lucas offered.

"That's a long way to the river for a small boy," Sam'l said.

"I'm not a small boy," Lucas responded angrily.

"Of course you're not, but I can't let you go, Lucas," Pa intervened. "I need you at home."

"Oh, I've surely made a real mess out of everything," Sarah wailed.

CHAPTER TWENTY-FIVE

EMMA SOLVES A PROBLEM

Sarah tossed and turned with pain. Adam went to the river and carried bucket after bucket of cool water so that Delia could bathe Sarah's sweaty body and try to ease the fever and the agony of the broken arm.

"You feed the babies, Delia. I'll keep a cool cloth on her head and see that she keeps her arm still," Adam said. "Luke, Sam'l and Lucas can finish up the chimney without me now. This will give us a chance to talk. I've been wondering when I'd have a chance to talk to you alone."

"What do you have on your mind, Adam? I thought something was worrying you."

"It appears that I'm going into business after all. This opportunity with Ike and the bricks is just too good to turn down. I'm not sure that I'm ready to get that tied down," Adam replied.

"Maybe Nathan or Lucas would be interested."

"No, Nathan is already gone and Lucas wants to go farther west. It's getting too crowded for them in these parts, they say. I'm concerned about Luke. After all he's done for our family, I feel a responsibility to him. He's not getting any younger, and I've noticed his favoring the leg that he froze several years ago. Then there's Sarah. She should have a chance to be more than a housekeeper for her father and the boys."

"She's such a delightful and busy person," Delia said. "She'd make someone a wonderful wife."

"Yes, she would," Adam agreed. "Oh, here come the others now. We'll talk more a bit later."

"How's Sarah?" Luke asked.

"She's finally asleep," Delia said. "It's a good thing she brought those medicine herbs. Who'd have thought we'd have to use them first for her?"

"That's a painful break she has," Luke said. "I hope I set it right. She won't use that arm for a while."

"She's more upset about being useless than she is about the pain," Adam added, "She feels like she let everyone down."

"We'll make out. It won't be easy. We all depend so much on her that we don't realize how much she does. We forget how young she is. Guess this accident will teach us a lesson," Luke said.

"I'll help take care of her like she cared for me when my leg was broke." Lucas rarely talked. Now, he felt that he had to offer his aid for Sarah. Maybe, in a small way, he could pay his debt of care to her.

"Well, the first thing to do is to get her home with as little pain as possible. She sure can't carry anything, and we'll have to take it slow," Luke said.

"Do you think we could carry her on a litter?" Adam asked.

"She'd never hear of that. She'd say it isn't her leg that's broken, it's her arm," Delia said.

"It would be helpful if we could make it from here to the fort in one day. Then she could rest at Martha's before we went all the way home," Luke said.

"Pa, if you are worried about Ike, I could go on ahead and help out at home," Lucas said.

"Lucas, I really appreciate your suggestions, but I'd rather that we all would travel together."

"It's a long journey to your place, Luke. Do you think you should leave so early?" asked Sam'l.

"I ain't worried as much how to get her home as what to do with her when she gets there. She'll want to get to work. She'll be cleanin' the cabin like she was killin' snakes. That won't help that arm heal," Luke worried.

Emma came in from tending the babies. She quietly slipped over to Delia and whispered in her ear. Delia nodded and smiled and hugged Emma.

"Emma has a solution to your problem," Delia announced. "She's offered to go with you to help Sarah. I can take care of the babies alone. Both of my arms work. She and Sarah are friends already."

"Are you sure you can do without her?" questioned Luke.

"I will miss her, but Sarah needs her more than I do."

It was settled. As soon as Sarah could travel, thought Luke, Emma would leave with them. It would be nice to have Emma around for a while—she was such a nice, quiet person.

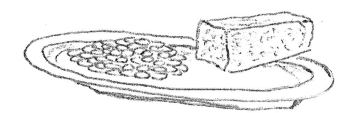

CHAPTER TWENTY-SIX

TIME TO GO HOME

"Pa, my arm don't hurt as bad as it has. I think we need to get home. Ike's probably made mud tracks all over the cabin floor."

"Yes, I think we'll leave in the morning."

"I need to tend to the garden. Ike don't act like it would bother him if the gourds rooted or the weeds took over the pumpkins," Sarah continued.

Patiently, Luke responded, "I know, Sarah. But Ike ain't there to keep house." He turned to Sam'l and said, "Yes, I think we better leave in the morning. We don't want to eat Delia and Sam'l out of their supplies."

"That ain't likely, Luke," Sam'l replied. "In the last two days, you and Lucas hunted enough to keep us fed all winter—and then some. It's all salted or larded away and ready for when we need it."

At daybreak, after a tearful farewell to Delia and the babies, Sarah fell into line. The procession moved away from the cabin in single file. Luke led, followed by Lucas, then Emma, who was followed by Sarah, while Adam brought up the rear. They wanted to make it to the settlement as soon as possible.

It was a long walk, punctuated with rest stops for Sarah. She would never ask to rest, so Adam would call a halt whenever he sensed that Sarah was tiring. As they walked, Adam was gaining a new appreciation of Sarah. He realized how unselfish she was.

"Sarah," Adam said, "I think I'll join Ike in the brick making venture."

Sarah wasn't surprised. She answered. "Adam, I think that is a good idea. There are many problems starting a new venture, but I believe you can do it. What do you plan to do with your claim?"

"I reckon I'll have to grow a crop in order to keep it, but it doesn't have to be a big crop. I can plant a field of corn and a garden."

"I can help you prepare your food for the winter. Of course, I will have to wait until my arm heals and I can use it again."

"Oh, Sarah, I can't let you do that. You have enough work to do at your own place."

"Yes, Adam, I do have plenty of work, and with Nathan coming back soon there will be more, but if you are to start a brick making venture, you will need some help. I would suggest you take your meals with us whenever you have to go to the brick works."

"Sarah, don't you think you are extending yourself pretty far?"

"Yes, I also know that. I do feel, though, that with Emma's help I can manage to cook, and one more person to feed would make no difference."

In no time, they approached the fort. Sarah was glad they were stopping for overnight. She didn't know if she would be ready to travel the next day, as her arm hurt frightfully.

ℬ

Sarah slept late the morning that they arrived at the settlement, and Luke and Adam visited old friends. Adam told several people about the brick works and asked what they thought of the idea. Most men were in favor of building the sidewalls of the new cabins with brick, as they felt the bricks would be stronger and more airtight than logs. The bricks would be easier to manage. Adam was feeling cheerful that the idea was met with some positive response and even a few helpful suggestions. Later in the day, he visited Sarah.

"Is your arm feeling better today, Sarah?" he asked.

"Yes, Adam. At first, I didn't think I would need a day of rest, but I truly did. I hope I didn't slow up all of us getting home."

"We can leave early tomorrow morning and be at your home by nightfall."

"What about you, Adam, are you going to our cabin, too?"

"I plan to, Sarah, I'd like to see all of you home, and then I can go to my cabin."

"But you can stay overnight, can't you?"

"I reckon I can. I'd like to visit with Ike as well."

§

The next morning, Luke led the group, again followed by Lucas and then Emma. Sarah and Adam were walking side by side at the rear, engaged in conversation.

"Tell me about living back East, Adam," she asked.

Adam gave her a long explanation of city living in Boston and the difference between Boston and wilderness living in Kentucky County. At the end of his lecture, Sarah sighed and concluded that she would rather live on the frontier. She wished that there could be more music and more opportunities to learn. Other than that, though, she thought Kentucky was a perfect place.

"Sarah," Adam said, "I'd be willing to share my books with you. I can tutor you in history and mathematics."

"I would so appreciate that, Adam."

It seemed to Sarah that they had hardly left the fort when they arrived at their own clearing. Although she had walked steadily all day, she was not tired. She felt an exuberance and hopefulness at the prospect of Adam tutoring her. She was beginning to feel very close to Adam

Arriving at their cabin, Sarah was amazed that the place was quite clean. Either Ike hadn't dirtied it up too much or he had cleaned. She felt that she had enough energy to scrub the floor. Unfortunately, her useless arm kept her from doing so.

Over the evening meal that Emma and Sarah had made, the family reflected on their good fortune. Sarah felt she was right where she belonged, surrounded by those she loved.

Lucas had been unusually quiet on the trip from Sam'l's place. He had been thinking about Nathan and realized how much he missed him. He was also aware that Sarah and Adam had a running dialog all the way from the fort. Emma, on the other hand, had been about as quiet as Lucas. She seemed like a lost girl who had been moved around at someone else's convenience.

It was true, she had been. Orphaned at the fort, sent from Martha's to Delia's and now to Sarah's cabin. She was beginning to wonder if she would ever find a permanent place.

CHAPTER TWENTY-SEVEN

THE BIG RIVER

"Robert!" David called.

"Yes, David," answered Robert, gently.

"We been walking close to a week now. Are you sure that we can find the river?"

"David, the river flows from the east to the west. We are walking north. Some day we will cross it—I mean, we will come to it. I don't know when—but within a day or so, I would guess."

"It's late. We can camp here for the night and push on tomorrow," Nathan added.

And so the three boys made camp. They had shot a rabbit and field dressed it early in the afternoon. They all had special tasks to do when they set up camp. Nathan set about to clean and divide the rabbit. David gathered wood for the fire, while Robert took his flint and started a small blaze. Soon, the fire was burning and they set out to roast the rabbit. As usual, the conversation was about an uncertain future that none of the boys could predict but all worried about.

"Robert, I ain't never worked for anyone else before. I don't quite know what to say," Nathan admitted.

"Well, I ain't, either. I know you look for the foreman of the place where they portage the material down the river and ask him for a job. I don't know how they pay, nor nothin' else."

"It's a worrisome thing, but we can't do nothing about it until we get there," David replied.

"I reckon we should get some sleep," Robert said.

✍

The next morning, the boys got up at sunup, stretched, and packed their gear. No one was talking. They had run out of food and there was no breakfast. The boys fell into a single file with Robert leading, followed by David and, finally, Nathan.

They walked until almost mid-morning. Robert, about ten yards ahead as they climbed a small hill, stopped, turned and excitedly called, "David, Nathan! Take a look!"

Before them stretched the Ohio River.

"Oh, man, is that a big river!" Nathan exclaimed.

The three boys stood, mouths agape, looking at the Ohio. "It's got to be a mile wide," David said.

"Well, it's not a mile wide, but it is wide," Robert corrected.

"I wonder which way the falls are? I would hate to walk the wrong direction for a day or two."

"Well, let me think. I think we should walk upstream. I think I saw some smoke coming from about a mile or so in that direction. Maybe someone there can tell us where the Falls are," Robert concluded.

"Good idea, Robert. Let's be off, then."

Again, Robert led the trio. He walked to the river's edge, turned upstream, and set off at a steady pace. They walked for about a mile—and then they could see the falls.

"What a magnificent sight," Robert said.

"It is breath-taking!" Nathan agreed.

"We are almost where we aimed to be some months ago, Robert," David chimed in. "I am truly excited."

As they approached the falls, they could see a crowd of people, about ten or fifteen of them. As they approached the group, a well dressed gentleman called, "Boys, boys, are you looking for work?"

"Yes, sir," Robert replied.

"We need these bags carried up the river to the dock. We will give you silver to carry them to the dock."

"We each can carry two bags going up. Will we get paid when we get to the top of the falls?" Robert asked.

"Yes, I will give you cash when we get to the dock."

"All right, boys, lets carry the bags up the river. This is our first job."

And so Robert, Nathan and David carried the bags up to the dock at the beginning of the falls. The gentleman gave the boys their money. Nathan had never seen money before. Robert had and said that it was genuine. He bit on it to make sure.

They looked around and spotted a man in work clothes who appeared to be the foreman. They approached him and Robert, again the spokesman, stated their desire to work. The foreman was a robust and jovial man who said, "I would be happy to let you three work for me. Strong help is hard to get. Most people who come here are looking to settle a claim and move on. I will pay you for transporting cargo both up and down the falls. If you want, you can contract separately to carry baggage for the passengers. I won't pay you for that, but I will pay you for the work you do for me."

The three boys agreed to work for the foreman, who went by the name of Jake. Jake showed them a tent and said they could put their gear inside the tent and they could sleep in it. They would have to get their own food, though, or buy it from one of the vendors who had stands near the dock.

That evening, sitting around their campfire, the three young adventurers felt quite smug about finding the river and getting a paid job the very first day. Would things go this easy while they were here and under Jake's the supervision? Maybe that would be too easy.

CHAPTER TWENTY-EIGHT

A SHORT SUMMER

Nathan, Robert and David worked most of the summer, portaging cargo down the falls and then portaging other cargo back up. The work wasn't steady, though. Some days they would work many hours, but on other days nothing would be going either up or down the river. However, on the slow days they were not able to leave the campsite, as something *could* appear. Besides, they had promised Jake to be responsible for all the cargo, and so Jake didn't hire anyone else for the job.

For the most part, the boys took care of themselves with no interference from Jake. They either cooked their own food or sought out food in some of the eateries in the campsite. On Clark Island, near the base of the falls, there was a tent restaurant that offered a decent meal for five cents. One meal a day like that kept the boys well nourished.

One morning, Nathan noticed that the humid air was being replaced with a dryer, fall air that reminded him of his promise to Pa. He said to his fellow workers, "Boys, I have to go home and help Pa get the corn in."

Robert asked, "How long will it take to pick the corn?"

"With three of us picking—Pa, Lucas and me—it would only take several weeks. Depends upon the weather and what else Pa has to do."

"What if I came with you, Nathan? Would that help? It would add one more person to the work force—then we would be done sooner."

'What about you, David? Do you want to come along as well?"

"I don't believe I do. If it is all right with the two of you, I'll stay here and portage cargo. I don't know how to pick corn, nor do I want to make that long walk again. I'll be here when you get back."

"If that is settled and it's all right with Jake, we can start in the morning. It should be easier to get back to Pa's than it was coming here."

"It's agreeable with me if it is all right with David." Robert checked one more time. David nodded and said that he would hold down the tent and await their return.

℘

Early in the morning, Nathan and Robert set out. Nathan asked, "How long do you think it will take us going back?"

"It took us seven days to come here because we didn't know where we were going. I figure it will take five going back because we can walk at a steady pace and not waste much time trying to figure out where we are."

"For the most part, Robert, we can dead-reckon and get very close to either the fort or Pa's place."

They walked steadily from sunup until sundown for several days. They were making excellent progress until Nathan stepped into a hole and severely hurt his leg.

Robert saw him fall and cried, "Nathan, are you hurt?"

Nathan couldn't answer at first, the pain was so great. Finally, he gasped, "Robert, I've really hurt myself. I don't know if my leg is broke or sprained, but I can't stand on it."

"What are we going to do, Nathan? I know I can't carry you. Should I try to fix a crutch? What should I do?"

"I'm afraid I am going to be a burden. I think you can fix me a campfire, lay out my bed roll, and then I think that if you take off just a little to the southeast you will get to some place with people either late tonight or early tomorrow morning. See if you can get some men to come and get me. I know I can't walk. We should be kinda close to the fort."

"How will I find you again? I don't know these woods like you do."

"Well, somehow you have to mark your trail, either with a broken stick or small piles of rocks that will point you back this way."

Robert laid out Nathan's bedroll and helped him on it. He set up a campfire that Nathan could feed any time he needed to, and he hacked a tree limb into a sort of crutch. Then Robert set out on a course for the fort.

Robert walked as fast as he could and even jogged in some open places. He was fearful of leaving Nathan out alone and helpless for all night. It soon became dark and Robert had to make camp. He realized that he had nothing to eat, so he just rolled up in his bedroll and went to sleep.

By mid-morning the next day he came upon a cabin. The settlers directed him to the fort. Once there, he set about getting a rescue team to go after Nathan.

CHAPTER TWENTY-NINE

UNEXPECTED RESCUE

"Nathan, Nathan, wake up."

Nathan sat up as best he could. He opened his eyes in surprise. "Running Deer! What are you doing here?"

"My name is now Ezra Running Deer," the Indian said, proudly. "We are scouts for the U.S. Army."

Nathan looked around and saw two more Indian braves. Nathan's spirits sagged as he remembered his time in the Indian camp. "What are you going to do with me this time, Running Deer?"

"I have new name, Ezra, and was baptized as a Christian. No capture any more. Running Deer must take you to his camp. Your leg is hurt too bad for you to stay out in the woods."

"I don't want to be a slave in an Indian camp again, Running Deer."

"I am no longer part of a big camp," Running Deer insisted, "there are just the three of us who are scouts. We no longer belong to Shawnee village." He gestured to his two colleagues but did not introduce them to Nathan.

"Nathan, you must listen. We can fix a litter for you and take you to our camp, which is not too far from here. We will care for you until you are better, then you can go to the fort or your home. We not capture you."

The Indians fashioned a litter, put Nathan and all his belongings on it, and proceeded through the woods. It was a mile or so to the campsite of the person he knew as Running Deer.

By mid afternoon, Robert, James and two other men arrived at the campsite where Robert had left Nathan. When they arrived, they were surprised to find that Nathan was not there.

"Are you sure this is the place where you left him?" James asked.

"I'm positive. Here is the campfire; here is the hole he stepped in. I am absolutely positive," Robert answered.

"I can't tell which way he went; there are signs leading off in several directions," James said.

"Do you suppose he went home?" one of the other men asked.

"I don't see how—he couldn't walk. Maybe someone came along and took him to the fort on another trail," Robert answered.

"I don't see any answer except to go back to the fort," James said.

"I don't know what to do," Robert said. "Maybe I should go back to the River Falls. I need to be with my brother."

"I understand how you feel, Robert. I suppose that is a good course of action for you. We'll head back to the fort. Then, if we don't find him there, one of us will go and find Luke and tell him. We can get a group of men together to search for him."

"If you find Nathan, tell him that David and I will be at the Ohio River Falls. We will wait there. That is where our work is."

Immediately, Robert started for the falls and James and his party headed back to the fort to do what they had to do.

Nathan was alive, they were sure of that—but where?

CHAPTER THIRTY

NEW PLANS

"That surely is the least talkin' girl I've ever seen," observed Luke as he dropped an armload of wood on the porch. "If I didn't hear her talkin' to you, Sarah, I'd think she didn't know how."

"Pa, you have to understand that she is alone. There's nobody left of her family. She told me that she doesn't know where she will go when my arm is better. She sure has been a big help to me. We've got the onions strung and all the beans dried. The potatoes are ready to go into the fruit cellar, and . . ."

"Wait a minute, Sarah. We ain't got a fruit cellar."

"Oh, didn't I tell you? Adam's coming over to help dig one for me. He's got a plan for one in his journal. He's got a plan for a spring house, too. Now that we have goats, I'll need a place to keep the milk cooled, and the cheese," Sarah said.

"Do you know how to make cheese?" Luke asked.

"No, but Adam has a book on making cheese."

"Is there anything Adam don't have a book on?" Luke laughed.

"Not that I am aware of," Sarah smiled.

"Tell me, Sarah, you and Adam spend a lot of time together. Is there anything I should know?"

"Like what, Pa?" Sarah answered, coyly.

"Like, are you two holding hands?' Luke asked directly.

"Oh, Pa, I'm terribly fond of Adam. I don't know his intentions. He hasn't said anything." Sarah blushed.

"I know that you are becoming a very pretty young woman, Sarah. I know that Adam could use a wife, and I also know that the two of you are very good friends."

"Yes, Pa, we are," Sarah conceded.

"As for Emma, she's not to worry that we'll turn her out. She sure has been a big help to us," Luke said. "She's good company for you, too. It's hard to be without a woman for you to talk to. I know how much I looked forward to Sam'l's visits when you all were young. Now I have Adam close by for man talk. Nathan is coming back soon, and Lucas is here.

Just then Lucas poked his head in the cabin door. "Pa, I'm going to see if I can get a deer. We need some skins for making moccasins for Emma and a dress like Sarah's. Emma told me she'd make me some jerky from the meat if Sarah'd teach her how to do it."

"That's good thinkin', Lucas. I guess it's time to get our meat ready for cold weather. We need to catch some fish for smoking as well."

Lucas got the rifle and left in search of a deer. Luke and Sarah looked at each other. It seemed that Emma was becoming more integrated into the family, and it seemed certain that she would stay with them for the winter and assume her share of the responsibilities.

"I really should start picking some corn within the next few days. I wonder when Nathan will be back? I truly miss the boy."

"So do I, Pa. I never thought I would say that. He was such a messy person to have around, but I really miss him, and I know Lucas does, too."

"It seems like ever since we came to Kentucky County we have had someone new move in and become part of our family. Lucas and Suzanna stayed the longest," Pa mused.

"Suzanna . . . I haven't thought of Suzanna in a while. I wonder where Jacob and Suzanna are. I suppose they are at the fort. I wonder how their new store is doing."

"I don't know, Sarah, I don't know." Luke's thoughts strayed on to his farm duties.

Sarah's thoughts, though, were a little more serious. Now that Emma would be staying for the winter and possibly longer, she could answer the question that Adam had proposed. She could leave the homestead without feeling guilty about leaving Pa and the boys. Emma would have a place where she belonged. Sarah would be close enough to help her with things that she hadn't learned yet. When Adam arrived today, she could tell him that she would be his wife when the first greens came up in the spring. They would start their own traditions. She would have a reason to wear the watch that Sam'l had given her. It would be the 'old' that she should wear on her wedding day. Meanwhile, she had much to do. She would be sure to leave Pa's cabin as clean as she could.

CHAPTER THIRTY-ONE

THE RETURN

"Pa! Pa! Can you help me?"

Luke looked up to see Nathan just starting across the clearing. "Nathan! Oh, my boy, what happened to you?'

"I was coming home with Robert and I stepped into a hole and hurt my knee real bad."

"I knew you were hurt. Some men from the fort came by and told how Robert came to the fort for help. They went back with him and you had disappeared. What happened, son?"

"This you are going to find hard to believe. Running Deer found me. He and two other braves found me and took me back to their campsite deep in the woods."

"You mean, Running Deer took you back to the Shawnee camp?"

"No, Pa, Running Deer and these other two left the Shawnees. They got jobs being scouts for the U.S. Army."

"Where do they live?"

"Pa, I really can't tell you. I don't know, because I was delirious when they found me. I don't remember much on how we got to their camp. What I remember is, there were three squaws there and they had made several shelters. I stayed in one shelter. The squaws made a God-awful smelly poultice for my leg. I just laid there for a week or so."

"You've been unaccounted for about three weeks. We were so worried. We almost gave up on you."

"Where is Robert? I know he was going to the fort. Did he stay at the fort?"

"No. According to the men who came out, he went back to the river to work and be with his brother."

"Pa, I can hardly walk, but I think I can help pick corn."

"Nathan, Lucas and I are doing quite well. We won't need you to pick corn until your leg is healed a little better."

"Thank you, Pa. I do feel poorly."

"Nathan, how did you get here if you can hardly walk?"

"Running Deer and another brave brought me to the edge of the clearing. Pa, you won't believe the change in Running Deer. He speaks pretty good English, and he is very kind and gentle."

"I find that hard to believe."

"I know, Pa. I found it hard to believe myself."

"Does he still think of himself as an Indian?"

"Yes, he does. We talked about that, but he can't remember not being an Indian. He is confused now because he can't go back to the Shawnee—nor can he live with the whites."

Sarah came out of the cabin and was surprised to see Nathan. "Nathan! Nathan!" she called. "Oh, my, we were so worried."

"Running Deer rescued Nathan and cared for him and brought him back to the edge of the clearing," Luke explained.

"Running Deer?" Sarah was bewildered.

"Yes, Running Deer," Nathan replied. "He rescued me in the woods and cared for me until my knee was almost ready to support my weight. Then he and another brave helped me get to the edge of the clearing."

"Oh, God! Where is he now?" Sarah's old fears returned.

"I reckon he has headed back. He said he wasn't ready to face Pa yet."

"Yet?" Sarah said.

"Sarah, I feel differently about Running Deer now. He and his squaw were very kind to me. I don't know how to repay that kindness."

"Well, I don't want anything to do with Running Deer! I don't want him on this place! Pa, don't you let Running Deer near this place!" Sarah was furious.

"I'm sorry you feel that way . . ." Nathan started to say, but Lucas interrupted, walking up to the trio.

"Hello, Lucas—I finally got back."

"So I see." Lucas said, dispassionately.

"Pa, I've got lots to tell you, and I've got some silver that I saved from my work, but I need to sit down and rest my knee."

"Let's all go over by the dogtrot and sit down. I'd like to hear about the Ohio River and how you earned the silver. And what are we going to do with the silver anyway?"

"For one thing, you can go to the fort and trade silver for goods that you need. What we did was carry cargo up and down the Ohio River Falls. It was hard work some days, and other days there was nothing to do."

"Are you going back, Nathan?" asked Lucas.

"I don't see how I can go back before winter, but I would like to go back in the spring."

"I don't suppose you would take me this time, would you Nathan?"

"We'll have to wait until spring, Lucas, we'll just have to wait till then."

ABOUT THE AUTHORS

Elizabeth Durbin is a retired teacher. She was born in Wisconsin and, because her father was an army officer, the family moved often, settling finally in Bowling Green, Kentucky, where Betty earned both bachelor's and master's degrees in education at Western Kentucky University.

After teaching at the university for a year, Betty began a series of assignments at military bases, first at Fort Knox, Kentucky and then at Mannheim, Germany.

Returning to the States, she taught in California and back in Kentucky for the last 24 years of her career. Her specialties were Art and English.

A mother of six, Betty first told stories then committed them to writing so her children could read them.

She lives full-time in Bowling Green but spends summers at a cabin at Barren River Lake, Kentucky, a home she built from the ground up.

Ernest Matuschka, a Nebraskan, grew up in a small town, which afforded him the opportunity to hunt and fish throughout his youth.

Shortly after graduation from college, he entered the U.S. Air Force—during the Korean war—where he served as an intelligence officer.

Following his military service, he taught school in Colorado, in California and in Paris, France, where he was a guidance counselor, and later moved to Germany, where he served as Director of Guidance at the Mannheim American School.

It was in Germany that he met his writing partner, Elizabeth Durbin. The Durbins and the Matuschkas had ten children between them, and they (and their families) became fast friends during the two years they were together. The Matuschkas returned to California at the end of their German experience, and, a few years later, Ernest applied for a leave of absence to complete work on his Ph.D. in clinical psychology. When he earned that degree, he and his family returned to Nebraska, where Ernest took a teaching position at the University of Nebraska at Kearney and opened a small, private practice. Ernest has written a number of professional articles for peer review psychology journals, authored two books on genealogy, and translated a book from German to English. He retired from teaching and from practice in 1990. With their children grown and gone, the couple has spent the last decade living half time in Nebraska and half time in Chandler, Arizona.

ᚠ

Cole Matuschka, who produced the interior text illustrations for this book, is a freelance artist in Sellersburg, Indiana, where he lives with his parents and one brother. He intends to follow his passion for art by pursuing a degree at nearby Indiana University Southeast.

Ashley Durbin, illustrator of the cover, lives with her family in Newbern, Tennessee. A junior at Dyersburg High School, she plans to attend the University of Tennessee at Knoxville upon graduation. Ashley has taken two years of visual arts classes, enjoys working in watercolor, pencil and woodcut, and is also an active member of the tennis team and Future Teachers of America.

For further information or to order additional copies of this book or others in the "Built to Last a Lifetime" series, please contact

OPA Publishing
Box 12354
Chandler, Arizona 85248-0023

Or visit the OPA Publishing web sites at
http://www.opapublishing.com/
or
http://www.opapresents.com/

opa

Printed in the United States
34444LVS00005B/127-135

9 780911 041361